THE PURLOINED LOVE

THE PURLOINED LOVE
An Inspector Canal Mystery

Bruce Fink

Any resemblance between Inspector Canal and actual persons,
living or dead, might well be intentional.
All other characters are substantially fictional.

KARNAC

First published in 2014 by
Karnac Books Ltd
118 Finchley Road
London NW3 5HT

British Library Cataloguing in Publication Data

A C.I.P. for this book is available from the British Library

ISBN-13: 978-1-78220-085-7

Typeset by V Publishing Solutions Pvt Ltd., Chennai, India

Printed in Great Britain

www.karnacbooks.com

They loved these things not because of each other but
each other because of these things.

—A letter writer

Heaven first taught letters for some wretch's aid,
Some banished lover, or some captive maid;
They live, they speak, they breathe what love inspires ...

—Alexander Pope

The late-afternoon sun glistened in Hélissenne's hair as her
one-handed pickax struck something that made a sound unlike
any she had ever heard. The ardent young woman had been
spending the summer with a group of budding archeologists
exploring every nook and cranny of Puilaurens—an eerie, forbidding twelfth-century Cathar castle perched atop a densely
wooded mountain in the foothills of the Pyrenees—and the
recent monotony of their finds had begun to take a toll on her
usually buoyant spirits.

Not five minutes before, the Frenchwoman had been
muttering to herself, *"Toujours la même chose,"* as she chipped

1

away yet another piece of a mullion window jamb from the medieval stone and mortar foundations she had unearthed day after day, but this hollow sound was quite distinctive. She shined her flashlight into the tiny hole she had made in the mortar around the stonework she had been exploring, and it shone back at her, reflecting off what was clearly a polished surface of some kind.

With heart pounding, she was about to deliver a few carefully aimed blows of the pickax to the adjacent cement-like material when a chorus of voices reached her—her fellow interns telling her it was time to knock off for the day and head home. If she didn't return with the motley crew of mostly European volunteers, there would be no ride back to the nearby town of Lapradelle. So she quickly took a couple of photos of the general area she had been working on, jammed her camera in her shoulder bag, and reluctantly ran to join the others for the twenty-minute hike back down the mountain to the van waiting for them at the visitor center.

Hélissenne's first inclination was to share her excitement about the potentially significant find with her best friend Isabeau—well, her real name was Isabelle, but everyone had been calling her by the more ancient form of her name since she had become enamored of the Middle Ages in high school. Isabeau had chosen the same summer internship offered by their graduate program in medieval studies in Poitiers, a medium-sized town in central western France. But Hélissenne recalled Isabeau's increasing jealousy of her of late for having a boyfriend and her occasional quips about Hélissenne being too brainy for her own good and luckier than anyone else at the dig in finding significant artifacts. Why bother to rekindle her jealousy when it might, in fact, turn out to be nothing at all?

In any case, Lizella, one of the other interns, monopolized the conversation, as she almost always did, and Hélissenne ended up telling herself that she might as well wait until she could confirm it wasn't merely a piece of glass or even just a stone containing a good deal of mica. More than a little competitiveness had manifested itself among certain members of their so-called team, especially among the graduate students from the Anglo-Saxon world, competitiveness she could barely understand given the somewhat thankless nature of their collective endeavor. But there it was all the same. Perhaps it would be better, she told herself, to keep mum today than to expose herself to ridicule tomorrow. Not that she had ever been exposed to much, having always acted and spoken prudently beyond her years.

During the steep hike, which she could now do both up and down virtually in her sleep, so often had she scaled this particular mountain, Hélissenne turned over in her mind the different possibilities of what she had seen. By the time she reached the van, she was lost in thought.

I

Hélissenne exited the dormitory-like hotel the interns were lodged in, having showered, primped, and changed. Her heart pounding in anticipation, she virtually skipped over to the nearby sidewalk café where she was to meet her boyfriend of recent date. He, a tall, tousle-haired, square-jawed American named Geoffrey, was already there, sitting in front of a horrible looking *menthe à l'eau*—a kind of sickly sweet mint syrup he would drink endlessly, adding water to it every few minutes—his nose in a small hardcover Loeb classics volume.

"Ave Hélissenne," he greeted her, smiling broadly, standing up to kiss and hug her.

If their widely divergent backgrounds weren't enough to make them an unlikely couple, a further obstacle lay in the fact that he spoke almost no French—even her name was virtually unpronounceable for him. He had resorted to calling her Helly-Seine, since he could pronounce the name of the famous river running through Paris but could not stop himself from pronouncing the silent H at the beginning of her name. And she spoke virtually no English, even though she understood some of the basics and could painstakingly decipher articles in her field written in English when she had to. The sole language they both knew tolerably well was Latin, and it was her command of medieval Latin and his grasp of Cicero's Latin that had allowed him to flirt in such an unheralded manner with the pretty girl he had noticed during his unguided tour of the portions of the Puilaurens castle that were open to the general public.

On the day of Geoffrey's visit, which was but one stop on a whirlwind tour of the formerly Latin-speaking parts of Europe he was making as if it might be his last, the girl had appeared to be rather preoccupied with her excavations. Toiling on the other side of the rope that set the dig area off from the visitable areas, she had struck him as quite fetching despite—or was it because of?—the fact that he could see nothing but her dust-covered face, the rest of her supple body being protected from the intense July sun by light-colored clothing.

Moseying over to the rope barrier, he had accosted her with one of the few French words he could pronounce approximately enough, *"Bonjour,"* but had been unable to make head nor tail of her reply, short though it had been. Noting his perplexity, and thinking she had detected an American accent in his greeting to her, she had stood up in a graceful manner unexpected in one so soiled, and added, "Good day." His attempt to engage her in further conversation with the casually pronounced words, "Find anything interesting today?" fell, however, not on deaf ears, for she was far from deaf, but on uncomprehending ones. Repeating them more slowly and articulating them more clearly led to no better results, but Geoffrey had refused to give up so easily. Figuring that he might be able to carry on some semblance of a conversation with the German he had learned in high school and was expected to know as a graduate student in classics at Yale, he had asked, *"Sprechen sie Deutsche?"* *"Nein,"* she had replied, shaking her head to supply additional comprehensibility to her vocalization.

Latin, the language he had spent the lion's share of his time studying in recent years, struck him as useless for anything but academic work, but as the only alternative was pig Latin, he had tried proffering, "*Caldarius hodiernus dies*" (awfully hot today). The surprisingly patient, lissome girl—who was by then standing upright in a marvelously poised posture, unlike so many of the coeds he had seen with hunched shoulders and drooping necks—had immediately smiled and responded, "*Et humidus nimis*" (and humid too). Although his pronunciation of Latin was typically American and hers typically French, they had managed to catch each other's drift. It was fun and intriguing to speak such an unusual language together and gave them the feeling of being in a world all their own.

Geoffrey was soon visiting the same Cathar castle almost every afternoon. He had changed his earlier plans to visit the mythic Quéribus one day, Foix another, Peyrepertuse yet another, staying in different towns almost every night, and had taken up quarters in a comfortable hotel in the tiny village of Gincla two miles south of Puilaurens. Their conversations across the rope barrier had lasted a little bit longer each day until most of a week had passed. Geoffrey was in no hurry, nor would anyone ever have dreamt of dubbing him a smooth operator.

Hélissenne was aware that this stranger, who gazed at her in a manner unlike that of any of the French boys she had known (the more interested in her they were, the more aggressive they tended to be) and who even stood differently from anyone she had ever met, probably was not returning day after day to the same site simply because of the unusual battlements and awe-inspiring view. She had often noticed him looking her way from various points around the castle courtyard and ramparts and suspected that he prolonged his visits until he could catch her alone, for he did not seem to dare to approach her when anyone else was nearby. Still she bided her time even as she noticed herself looking forward to their pourparlers, and frequently caught herself, around the hour of his usual afternoon passage, scanning the tourists as they trickled in through

7

the old portcullis, most of them puffing like steam engines as they tried to catch their breath after the steep climb. Geoffrey always appeared—but never when she was looking for him, somehow—and finally *ad prandium invitare*, asked her to lunch at his hotel in Gincla, fearing he would not see her the next day, as it was a Sunday. Hélissenne had accepted unhesitatingly.

They had painstakingly worked out the details of where Geoffrey would pick her up in his rental car—Hélissenne had to print the name of her hotel and its address in block letters on a piece of paper for him, his auditory comprehension of even simple French names and numbers being so woefully inadequate—and their lunch date had extended into a languorous hike in the surrounding mountains. It was soon followed by numerous other meals and walks and prolonged conversations in Latin interspersed with French and English words for which they could find no ancient corollary. Hélissenne had soon fallen in love with this curious man from the vast American Midwest, and Geoffrey—whom she called Geoffroi, being unable to pronounce Chaucer's first name like the English—had fallen in love with a lovely Poitevine, which meant, as he learned, a woman from the area around a town he had never heard of: Poitiers.

As she approached him now at the outdoor café, Geoffrey could see that Hélissenne was preoccupied. He stood up, wrapped her in his arms, and gave her a passionate kiss. Hearing her story of the possible find, he was so enthusiastic about it that he persuaded her to return to the site immediately with him to find out what it was. Initially reluctant to climb back up the mountain in the dark and work in the one remaining dress she had with her that was still presentable, she resisted his efforts at persuasion until he promised to supply flashlights and lend her protective outerwear—expressing the latter modern notions with a combination of English words and hand gestures, the gist of which she seemed to get.

II

Provisions for a moonlit picnic dinner were quickly cobbled together by Geoffrey at the local *charcuterie*, while Hélissenne retrieved tools and boots from her room. The two lovers were soon ascending the trail leading to the hushed, darkened castle perched atop the rugged peak. The ancient iron and wood portcullis having being closed at the end of the day, they had to circumvent the south and east walls along slippery, worn rocks to the opening near the easternmost tower, the door to which was almost always left unbolted, access to it being so precarious as to make locking unnecessary. Despite losing their footing here and there, and catching each other so as to prevent a potentially painful fall, the agile climbers made it to the east entrance with nary a scratch and entered the large, irregularly shaped courtyard drenched in the radiant light of the full moon.

Flashlights were no longer needed for them to find their way, and Hélissenne escorted Geoffrey directly to the spot she had photographed a few short hours before, the climb and excitement having cut their earlier appetite for food. As she removed the tools from her shoulder bag, she explained the particularity of the spot to him, for he knew little more about medieval castles than he had managed to glean in the course of the past six weeks in the southwest. This part of the courtyard had apparently been extensively revamped in the seventeenth century, when the castle was used as a military fort with which to defend the border between France and Spain. The spot she had been exploring was near current ground level, directly under a lintel that had supported the stonework above what had probably been a door or mullion window in medieval times.

Never the most attentive listener, Geoffrey was preoccupied with chipping away the mortar in the area Hélissenne had indicated, and interrupted her impassioned explanations with ohs and ahs whenever he saw light reflecting back to him from the hole. Hélissenne aborted her disquisition on the architectural history of the site and crouched next to Geoffrey to observe the progress of his work.

It was a box. Ecstatic that they had not been mistaken, they chattered animatedly as the opening grew and the outlines of a sizeable metal rectangle became visible to them. It had obviously been carefully cemented into place, for it took considerable chiseling and prying for them to extract it from its centuries-old cache.

But great was their disappointment when they found that the box was securely closed with a locking mechanism, the key to which they obviously did not have. Having attempted to pull it open with all of their combined strength a few times, Geoffrey proposed to smash it open with a rock or the pickax. Hélissenne raised a finger to stop him from performing so rash an act, as the contents might thereby be damaged, and felt around in her shoulder bag until she was able to fish out a hair pin. She tried it in the lock from every imaginable angle. "It always works in the movies," she explained, borrowing the last word from her limited English repertoire. Eventually tiring of the futile exercise, she laid the box down on the ground, and stood up, stretching. A bit of her earlier frustration with the mind-numbing tedium of the dig returned and she grumbled, "I should have known it wouldn't be that easy. I guess we'll have to find a locksmith who can—"

Her words were interrupted by a clicking sound.

She looked down to see Geoffrey lift the top of the box and asked admiringly, "How did you do it?"

"I simply tapped on your hairpin (this latter word in English) with the pickax and the lock sprang open."

Placing the box gently on the ground, Geoffrey gestured to Hélissenne that she should do the honors. Beneath the metal lid, lined, like the rest of the box, with what appeared to be cedar, she found a leather pouch, the laces of which she carefully yet deftly untied. Opening the pouch she felt inside and slowly removed a package wrapped in a rich, velvety fabric.

She abruptly placed the package back in the box. "I can't open it," she protested. "What if it contains the old bones of a saint? It would be too horrible to look at," she squealed, shuddering involuntarily.

"And you call yourself an archeologist?" Geoffrey retorted, teasing her.

"I only work with old stones, not old bones."

With Geoffrey, unwrapping the velvet packet was the work of not a moment but quite a few, as it turned out there were some embroidered fabric strips holding it together that he had not initially noticed, and manual dexterity with diminutive objects was not his forte.

When he had finally unknotted the strips and carefully peeled back each layer of velvet, two bundles of paper were revealed, one extremely old and brittle, the other still obviously quite old, but folded and tied up in a very different manner from the first. Ribbons held both bundles together and the overall appearance was of precious papers very carefully packed away for safekeeping.

"The parchment looks too old and delicate to examine here," Hélissenne opined, somewhat disappointed.

"I couldn't agree more," Geoffrey concurred, even as he shone the flashlight on the bottom page of the bundles that he had flipped over in his hand. "I can make out a few words," he said enthusiastically, *"Vale dulcissima. Totus tecum sum, et ut verius dicam, totus in te sum."*

"Are you translating, or is it really written in Latin?"

"It's really written in Latin, but the writing is very faded and difficult to make out. We'll need better lighting conditions and a magnifying glass and a ..." He began wrapping the papers in the velvet anew, but Hélissenne stopped him.

"Let me at least take a picture of the bundles as we found them and get a close-up of the top and bottom pages where the writing is exposed." Geoffrey placed the packet on a low-lying foundation wall and peeled back the material, while Hélissenne found her camera. She took a number of shots from several different angles, including the box and leather pouch in certain shots, after which Geoffrey turned the bundles over so she could take some close-ups.

When she signaled that she was done by turning off the camera, he began folding the documents in the fabric anew. He then handed the packet to Hélissenne, who placed it back in the leather pouch and then in the metal box. Geoffrey wrapped the box in a sweatshirt and stuffed it in his knapsack.

It was as if the significance of their actions suddenly hit Hélissenne and a certain nervousness swept over her. Looking up from her shoulder bag, in which she had just placed her tools, Hélissenne whispered, "What are we going to do about the hole?"

"Why would we do anything about it? Will anyone even notice? Aren't you the only one who works on this part of the site?"

"I think others would notice a hole as big as that," Hélissenne replied anxiously.

"Couldn't you just say that you'd opened up the mortar at the end of the day and found an empty space behind it?"

"I think the signs that something has been removed are too fresh right now—it would be obvious that someone had just taken something out of there," she continued, the first signs of panic manifesting themselves in her voice as she lapsed into French. *"Où avais-je la tête?* We have to bring the box directly to Monsieur Picard, the director of the dig. But how am I going to explain that I came up here at night? He already seems to dislike me, or maybe even distrust me, given those bizarre looks he gives me sometimes."

Geoffrey did his best to calm her down, realizing that her anxiously emphatic *aparté* in French meant she was losing it. After he had gotten her to explain the situation in plain Latin, he suggested, "Why don't we just put it back in the hole, and you can pretend to find it first thing Monday morning?"

"Yes, maybe that would be best," she assented. A few moments later, however, she added, "Unless someone else were to come along and …"

"And …"

"Swipe it."

"Swipe it?" Geoffrey echoed incredulously.

"Some of the other interns strike me as less than completely honest and of dubious integrity. You never know if I'll be the first person at the site the day after tomorrow, since not everybody comes in the van."

"They wouldn't simply give it to the site director?"

"I wouldn't put it past some of them to abscond with it," she replied, scarcely blaming them in her mind for failing to turn it over, Picard being a rather narrow-minded type whose taste for the Middle Ages was barely acquired, certainly not inspired, and whose only true passion seemed to be the seventeenth century, one of only tangential relevance to this particular archeological dig. He struck her as avaricious, wresting every artifact discovered by the interns from their sweaty hands the second he saw it and saving every penny possible on their room and board. He was even shifty in a way—quite different from the staid, stolid, intellectual kind she had encountered in the academy thus far. Hadn't she even heard him, she suddenly wondered, say something about a box? She couldn't recall whether it had been a few hours ago or a few days ago. Geoffrey's voice interrupted her meditations.

"So you think we should … " His voice trailed off.

"Abscond with it ourselves? Yes, I think that's the only thing we can do." Geoffrey nodded thoughtfully in assent, and then Hélissenne added, "That still leaves us with the problem of the hole."

Geoffrey looked around for a moment and then ordered, "Put a little dirt into the hole and jam this stone in there—it looks about the right size to me. I'll come up with something for the outside surface," he assured her.

Not feeling terribly reassured, nevertheless, Hélissenne began packing some of the dirt from the dig into the empty hole, feeling she didn't really have any other option. The stone fit rather well, as it turned out, and Geoffrey, who had ventured off to another part of the courtyard for a couple of minutes, returned with an unbroken portion of mortar that looked like it would fill the bill. He chiseled off little bits around the edge of it until it fit right over the hole that they had opened up with their blows. He wedged it securely into place, dusted off the entire area around it with his shirt sleeve, and then began to blow as hard as he could all around the area to remove any remaining sand.

Hélissenne stopped him after a few breaths, however, saying, "There's always dust and dirt around a dig—it's more likely to attract attention if it's freshly dusted than if it looks like everything else around here." She gestured to Geoffrey to stand back while she gathered a little dirt in her hands and threw it up in the air to let it scatter as it would in the gentle August breeze blowing on the mountaintop. She inspected the area around the hole again with her flashlight and, feeling satisfied with the result, led Geoffrey back toward the easternmost entrance.

14

III

Silence engulfed the lovers as they scrambled carefully around the southern battlements back toward the portcullis. It was only once they had reached the main trail that their tongues loosened.

"Vale dulcissima. Totus tecum sum, et ut verius dicam, totus in te sum," Geoffrey repeated aloud from memory, translating it to himself with relish as "Farewell, sweetest. I am wholly with you and, more truly put, I am wholly within you." Aloud he asked Hélissenne, "What do you make of that?"

"I was thinking about that too," she replied. "It sounds to me like the end of an elegant love letter written by a man to a woman. *Dulcissima,*" she added, with obvious delight.

"You mean, not like the kind I write to you?" Geoffrey retorted with feigned pique.

"You've never written me a single love letter."

"Of course I have. Well, I suppose they were actually more like Post-it notes, but I always express my love for you in them in the most urbane terms, unsurpassed in the *ars dictaminis.*"

"Yes, you sign your missives, 'Your impassioned Yankee.' You—"

"Shush," he hissed. "What was that?" he whispered.

"What was what?" she cried, bumping into Geoffrey who had abruptly come to a full stop in the middle of the trail.

"Hush," he hissed again, though more softly this time. "I thought I heard footsteps. They were coming from over there," he added, pointing to their right, where the trail wended its way among boulders and stone outcroppings.

Her gaze followed his index finger toward the rocks, and she cupped her hands behind her ears as if straining to hear. The only audible sound was that of their own breathing and of the gentle mountain breeze in the treetops.

"I didn't hear anything," Hélissenne finally murmured, leaning softly into his warm body.

"It must have been some pebbles we dislodged in passing, rolling down the hillside," he concluded. "We were over on that side just a moment before I heard it," he added, not responding to the physical contact, as if explaining the noise to himself more than to her.

She nodded and, noting his lack of response to her touch, was the first to resume their downward course. Geoffrey soon followed suit, but kept glancing for some minutes off to one side or the other of the trail, and listened less than attentively to Hélissenne's initial speculations.

"On the basis of this line, I would say," she opined, "that both the sender and the addressee must be well versed in letters, but the writer, at least, does not seem to be aware of Aquinas' critique of concupiscence-type love."

"Huh?"

"St. Thomas Aquinas."

"Yes, of course," said Geoffrey, who was not altogether ignorant of things scholastic. "What I didn't catch was that type of love you mentioned."

"*Concupiscentia*. It's the kind of love in which the lover wants to penetrate the beloved's heart and have it all for himself. He wants to completely monopolize her affections, such

16

that there will be no room for anyone else in her heart, whether friend or relative."

"Hmm," was the only response she received, and she wondered whether Geoffrey was still preoccupied with the sound he thought he had heard or whether it was just the widespread male tendency to listen to women with only one ear, if that, which was operative.

"For someone who could write such erudite prose, it would have been almost unthinkable not to know what Aquinas had said about the two loves, concupiscence versus friendship. Unless, of course, he was writing *before* the thirteenth century."

"Before what century?"

"Have you heard a single word I've said?"

"Yes, of course, of course. You were talking about love and possessiveness," the American replied in a pensive tone of voice. "Do you really think it's possible to not want all of your beloved's affections for yourself? If you're truly in love, don't you always want to be so essential to your beloved that her every thought is of you, her every joy comes from you, and that without you she has neither breath nor life?"

Hélissenne stopped dead in her tracks and Geoffrey collided with her on the narrow trail. She threw her arms around his neck, melted into his torso, and cooed, "That's awfully poetic, dearest Geoffroi." Then, with a more severe intonation, she added, *"Mais c'est très villain!* It's very naughty of you! You'll end up wishing me to be miserable without you, and that when you're away I be lifeless, breathlessly awaiting your return."

"But that is how it is, *dulcissima*," Geoffrey replied, holding her tight while trying to adopt a tone midway between dead seriousness and light-hearted banter, "I can't stand the thought of you enjoying yourself without me, of you having a good time when I am not around. I want you to be constantly preoccupied with me, and for there to be no room in your heart for anyone but me!"

Hélissenne examined his face pressed up close to hers in the moonlight and asked, "Not even Isabeau?"

He shook his head, refusing to grant Hélissenne's best friend any place in her heart.

"Not even Uncle Filbert?" she inquired breathlessly.

He shook his head again, adamantly barring all access to her affections to the man who had raised her since she was five.

"Not even François?"

"Especially not François," he replied resoundingly, jealous as he was of Hélissenne's former beau with whom she was now too chummy for his liking.

She looked deeply into his eyes. Both content with his response and troubled, she asked, "So you would have me all to yourself, regardless of how I feel about it?"

Sensing that he was heading into a potential minefield, despite the almost rhetorical nature of her question, Geoffrey backtracked, "How you feel is, of course, extremely important to me," he hurriedly whispered. "I want you to be happy, first and foremost," he concluded.

This response on his part spoiled the mood for both parties to the conversation—for Hélissenne because, although she believed this was what people were supposed to want for each other, she preferred the torrid passion implied by his desire to wrest her from all other comers and possess her exclusively—and for Geoffrey because he knew that what he had said simply wasn't true and felt he had retreated into the all-too-familiar position of lying to the one he loved.

They remained intertwined without any conviction now for a few false-hearted moments and then continued down the trail to Geoffrey's rental car parked in full view at the visitor center. As they pulled out, each was lost in private thoughts and silence enveloped them with its ever more impermeable shroud.

IV

Having dropped Hélissenne off at her hotel, Geoffrey drove slowly back to his own room in Gincla, brooding. He had hoped that things with this Frenchwoman were proceeding and would continue to progress differently than they had with the other women he had known and loved, or at least known—for he had often wondered what it meant to love and ended up berating himself, not for Alexander Pope's crime of loving too well, but of loving badly, if not simply confusing lust with love.

He was hardly a stranger to passionate relationships, having fallen head over heels on plenty of occasions in his thirty years of existence. But he had looked on helplessly, or so he told himself, as his passion for each girl had inexorably turned to dust—or rather, since he tried on this occasion to be honest with himself, to anger. Once the initial enthusiasm had worn off, he would invariably begin to feel that the girl he had fallen for was not really right for him, but he would stay with her nonetheless to be able to continue to have sex with her—that much he could easily admit to—but also out of an uncomfortable sense of dependency he was loath to examine in broad daylight.

Parking his car in the gated lot across from the hotel in the dark, he forced himself to go for a walk in order to reflect further. Despite being initially enamored of them, he had to confess to himself that girls always ended up becoming a refuge for him, a haven from the stresses of study and work. With them he could forget … Forget what? Forget himself, was the first answer that occurred to him. Forget his overweening ambitions came to mind next—his ambition to do something truly original, to do something no one else had ever done before, to distinguish himself from all others. He laughed inwardly, and hardly for the first time, at the absurdity of the project. However often he had heard that there was nothing new under the sun, he nevertheless believed that many of his professors had managed to break new ground and make original contributions despite the advanced age of their field.

His craving for originality had hardly begun with his study of classics. Arriving at the edge of the village and deciding to venture further south into the Pyrenees, Geoffrey reflected on his wish in his early teens to become a famous rock star by composing his own songs and innovating musically. "How unoriginal can you get," he exclaimed to himself, recalling his disappointment upon realizing that virtually all his friends and their brothers and sisters had the same fantasy.

His quest for originality hadn't stopped there, though. By his mid-teens he had moved on to other arenas and dreamt of becoming not just a thinker and social critic, but a philosopher who could reduce to silence every other philosopher with his dazzling argumentation, who could run dialectical circles around them, and whose way of thinking would revolutionize not just his contemporaries' conception of the world, not just the thinking of his century or even millennium, but would change the course of history for all time!

How devoid of substance it all now seemed. But the pressure he had put on himself to accomplish marvelous things by the age of sixteen and expose the fatal flaw in every other philosopher's claims by the age of twenty-five was anything but insubstantial. Treading the thin sliver of asphalt in the darkness, he asked himself if it had not, in fact, begun with his drive to contradict his parents in everything just for the sake of contradicting them, just to prove he was different from them. If so, it had certainly grown and expanded, turning into a quest for novelty for novelty's sake. It had weighed him down, spoiling his enjoyment of high school and college parties, and progressively sapping his joie de vivre.

Falling in love had been a welcome refuge from the pressure to innovate and, even after the initial infatuation had worn off, the comfort he felt in a girl's arms had been considerable. In running toward a girl who was running toward him, he had actually been running away from something, fleeing his own drive and hoping to lose himself in her. How Boethius could ever have penned *The Consolation of Philosophy* was beyond him. Had times really changed that much, he wondered, or was it just him? In his wish to become an earth-shattering philosopher, Geoffrey felt the need to be consoled about the stress he felt while pursuing philosophy. Philosophy had never served to console him in the slightest about anything whatsoever.

If only the solace he had sought from women could have truly consoled him once and for all! Lying in their arms he would soon begin thinking about his work-related ambitions again and would begin to resent the time he was spending with them and his all-too-obvious need for a sympathetic ear to pour his worries and concerns into. He hated himself for cravenly shying away from disputatious battle with his so-called peers and colleagues, all of whom he saw as rivals, to make the name for himself that he so desperately sought. Reluctant as he was to admit it to himself, he always made his girlfriends bear the brunt of his dissatisfaction with himself.

Angrier by the minute with himself, Geoffrey began striding faster as if to consume his rage. He almost fell after banging into an unseen rock that had rolled down the nearby slopes

21

onto the road. Cursing aloud, he was obliged to pause for a few moments as he took off his shoe and rubbed a throbbing toe, but then kicked the rock deliberately with the other foot.

Resuming his forced march, he pondered his inability to stop himself from taking out his self-loathing on whichever woman he was seeing at the time. Time spent with her quickly became of negligible importance compared to the great projects he felt he had to pursue. After an initial period in which he would find sex exciting and fulfilling, he would begin to see his own craving for it as fallen, deceitful, guilty, and even revolting at times—as both a thorn in his flesh and a kind of yoke. Showering meticulously thirty seconds after the completion of the act, images of Sartre's sordid sex scenes in *The Age of Reason* would flash through his mind, and he would recall Baudelaire's fateful description of "the rancid smell of desolation" after intercourse.

Replaying in his mind some such scenes with the girl he'd been seeing prior to Hélissenne, he realized that after taking his pleasure he would almost immediately find some trivial pretext for arguing with her. He'd explode in a temper and leave, slamming the door, as he escaped to his chaotic carrel at the university library—to get back to work, he told himself, but he usually frittered away the time thinking angry thoughts about his girlfriend instead.

Geoffrey shuddered at the recollection. Coming back to the present, he noticed that he had ventured far beyond the last streetlights of the village into an area where the crystalline moonlight of the clear summer night was hidden by the hulking mountain to his right. He made an abrupt about-face and directed his steps back toward the habitations.

Things with Hélissenne were different, for once, he now reminded himself. Hélissenne was someone with whom he could discuss philosophy and classics rather than escape from them. Her love for them bore little resemblance to his own— she was anything but argumentative with him and never

22

seemed to seek originality for its own sake, even though what she said often struck him as highly original. "The more you genuinely have to say," he concluded, "the less arrogant and self-aggrandizing you are. You simply allow your inventiveness to shine forth without feeling the need to shout it from every rooftop."

Ambling slowly now, he admitted to himself that he both hoped her calmer, saner attitude toward ideas would rub off on him and envied her unfeigned originality. Her passion for literature seemed unadulterated, whereas his merely adopted literature as a springboard for dazzling others with his dialectical prowess. When he allowed himself to indulge in anything other than schoolwork, he fantasized about growing potatoes, tilling the soil with his bare hands, or doing some other kind of physical labor that would take up all of his attention and exhaust his body—anything to take his mind off his philosophical ambitions.

Was he hoping, he wondered in a moment of cynical self-reflection, to hitch his wagon to her star and do something innovative through her? Did he imagine that her ideas might somehow fire or inspire his own? Or did he secretly wish to simply translate her reflections on medieval texts into a classical register and take credit for her insights? There was, he suspected, but one short step between admiration for her unassuming originality and out-and-out resentment. Would he end up playing Salieri to her Mozart?

If there was something that he felt he could congratulate himself for, it was not having rushed the sexual side of their relationship. He had at first been tempted to attribute his caution to some supposed decrease in his sex drive pursuant to his recent thirtieth birthday, but his repeated erotic dreams since he had met Hélissenne gave the lie to that ridiculous hypothesis. Her looks captivated him like no woman's ever had before, and her body exercised an irresistible gravitational pull on his that he could feel in his loins just by thinking about it.

If he had deferred sleeping with her, it was no doubt because he had a dim intimation of his tedious tendency to quickly shift from sexual passion for a girl to contempt for his own interest in sex, and subsequently for the female object of his interest. Hélissenne was the first girl whom he had not striven to sleep with early on, perhaps in the indistinct hope that the slippery slope toward dependency and resentment might be deferred in the absence of intimate relations, and that some other kind of relationship might be possible with this beguiling Frenchwoman. If nothing else, they conversed in Latin instead of in any kind of vernacular. And the language of their love was verbal, not physical—a first for Geoffrey—being that of Augustine, not Henry Miller or Mick Jagger. Perhaps, he conjectured optimistically, something new could grow out of this Latinate connection ...

V

Climbing the stairs to her room, Hélissenne gave free rein to her moody, silent musings that had begun during the car ride with Geoffrey back to the hotel. Although she had been fascinated by love as far back as she could remember, she had never truly been in love before. Despite having spent a fair amount of time with several different guys in her late teens and early twenties, she had always chafed at their possessiveness—they had wanted to control her and be party to every single one of her outings despite the fact that she just barely liked them enough to see them once in a while. Until Geoffrey had come along, she had never wished to belong to a man body and soul.

She adored everything about this American—his calmness, his insightfulness, his take-charge attitude, his profile … She even treasured his flaws, if they could be called such—the scar on his cheek, the meager handful of whiskers on his chin, his clumsiness with a knife. Everything in any way associated with him was a source of joy and wonder to her! She had even grown to like his hideous rental car and found herself looking affectionately at the horribly dirty hiking boots he'd left in her room one day.

The guys who had wanted her before had never struck her as men at all, merely boys. One might play games with boys, she reflected as she stepped into the shower down the hall to wash away the dirt from the dig, one might play at love, but her sole experience of love—if it could be called experience— prior to meeting Geoffrey was from movies and books. And although she had often been moved by the love stories portrayed in films and novels, and had gotten caught up in the excitement of certain heroines' passions, there was always something that never quite fit for her. Unlike so many of the girls and women depicted in cinema and literature, Hélissenne felt she would know when she was genuinely in love *not* the day she found a man handsome beyond words or courageous in the face of extraordinary danger, *not* the day she wanted to win him for herself, but the day she felt impelled to be everything for him.

She had read all the classical tales in which men spoke of being conquered by love, as if it had hit them from the outside, whether they invoked the trope of being struck by Cupid's arrow or burned by Eros' torch. But she had never felt that it would hit her all at once, like love at first sight, Stendhal's so-called thunderbolt. It seemed to her that love would involve a choice of some kind—a decision and a will on her part to make one man hers and to become his utterly and completely.

And while the literature of the sixteenth and seventeenth centuries—with its celebration by female authors of the joys of myriad flirtations, extramarital affairs, and surreptitious rendezvous—held no secrets for her, neither did it find any resonance within her. She had heard her girlfriends talk proudly of their conquests of this guy or that, as though men were mere feathers in their caps, or so many good catches to reel in and prepare for permanent display on the mantelpiece. Try as she might, she could not fathom how men could be viewed as trophies or possessions, for she herself wished to be the most prized possession of a man, to be altogether his.

To be besieged by myriad lovers was no fantasy of hers—her tastes were far more absolute than that. She dreamt of the burning intensity of devotion to her one and only, and this was what she had found with Geoffrey. He was constantly in her thoughts, so much so that she had been having a hard time thinking about anything else almost since the day they'd met. At the dig, she'd find herself endlessly scratching at the same bit of mortar without making a dent in it or catch herself staring off into space, lost in thoughts of Geoffrey. So large did he loom in her thoughts, there was no place for anyone else.

No, there could be no multiplicity of lovers for her. Unlike certain of her classmates, she had never sought to be surrounded by a gaggle of fawning, adoring admirers who might be meted out just enough attention to keep them around so she could feel special. Nor had she ever touted her noble family background or personal accomplishments so that guys would think her a suitable match or look to raise their own social standing in the world through her.

Until very recently, she would not have known exactly how to describe what she wanted in relation to a man. She thought of it mostly in terms of wishing to give herself to him body and soul, but when her girlfriends asked her what she wanted, they always couched their questions in terms of what *she* wanted from a man. All she could say was that she wanted to be taken by him, that she wanted him to consider her to be his absolutely, categorically, without remainder.

Hearing Geoffrey say he wanted to become the be-all and end-all of her existence—such that her every thought was of him and her every joy came from him, such that her very breath and life depended on him—had both thrilled her and disturbed her in some dimly perceived way.

"What bothers me about it?" she wondered as she stepped out of the shower and began to dry herself off with the plush bath towel she had brought from home, having little faith that a third-rate hotel such as this could provide anything she would be willing to press against her sensitive skin. Was it the mere fact of hearing her deepest wish spoken out loud? Or was it, rather, that Geoffrey seemed to want with her the very position that she wanted with him? He wanted to be everything to her—little did he know, he already was.

Did it make sense, she asked herself, that each partner wanted the same thing with respect to the other? It was an ideal she had often heard bandied about by people who wrote about love. But wasn't what she wanted an exclusive position that only one of the two partners could have vis-à-vis the other, that could not be shared?

Donning a sleeveless nightshirt and slipping between the sheets, she reflected that perhaps what Geoffrey had said he wanted only superficially overlapped with what she knew she wanted. Replaying his words in her mind, she realized that whereas he wanted to possess her, she wanted to be possessed by him, so perhaps their wishes were not incompatible after all ... Then, the double meaning of being possessed by someone suddenly struck her—what would it mean to be possessed by someone like Geoffrey, she asked herself. Should she be afraid of that? Was he a devil of some kind? Preoccupied by such questions, she fell into a fitful sleep.

VI

Hélissenne was in quite a state when Geoffrey came to pick her up the following morning to bring her back to his hotel, where they intended to peruse the letters they had brought to the light of day the previous night. Her room had been ransacked during breakfast! The lock had been forced, all her personal effects had been rifled through, every stick of furniture and every stitch of bedding had been turned upside down or taken apart, and all her pictures and posters had been ripped down and trampled on the floor.

"Whoever it was must have been looking for something very specific," she told Geoffrey, in anxious conclusion. "I'm afraid it was the letters they were after."

Although initially dumbfounded, Geoffrey quickly regained his aplomb. "At least those are safely tucked away," he reassured her, and then added, "But is there nothing else they might have been after? Don't you keep any valuables in your room?" As Hélissenne shook her head, he continued, "You didn't bring your camera down to breakfast with you, did you?"

"Of course not," she replied reflexively. Quickly opening her shoulder bag, she felt around until she had located the camera. "It's right here," she exclaimed triumphantly, obviously relieved.

"Is the memory stick still in there?" he asked.

Hélissenne opened the compartment and confirmed that it was.

"Why don't you turn it on just to make sure that the pictures you took last night haven't been erased?"

"I don't see how it could be the pictures they were after," she replied, but she scanned through the pictures anyway and reported that they were all there. "They must have been looking for something rather different to pull all the posters off my wall."

Geoffrey contemplated this for a few moments. "Maybe they were looking for a stash of cash, or a passport or driver's license—papers like that can fetch a pretty penny on the black market? Did you notice anything missing?"

"Weirdly enough, the only thing missing, besides a small amount of cash I had, is a knockoff Cartier watch my cousin gave me for my birthday, oh it must be ten years ago. It was sitting right next to my purse on the bureau, and even though the purse had been opened and its contents dumped on the floor, none of my papers were missing. I guess they couldn't tell the difference between a Cartier and a 'Catier'!"

They both laughed. On this lighter note, Geoffrey turned the key in the ignition and the reunited couple began their scenic journey to Geoffrey's hotel.

"So," Geoffrey concluded once they were en route, "we're either dealing with very stupid burglars or they were, as you suggested, after the letters. But who could possibly know about them already? You didn't mention them at breakfast to anyone, did you?"

"What, and get myself kicked out of the internship for absconding with state property? Hardly. It must have been someone who saw us or overheard us at some point last night. But all was quiet at the hotel when I got back last night. I don't think anyone could have seen me come in."

"Then maybe I wasn't imagining things when I thought I heard someone on the trail last night," Geoffrey said, feeling vindicated.

"No, maybe not. Perhaps someone saw me leave the hotel the second time with my hiking boots and archeology gear. It seems to me it has to be somebody who knows me and works at the same site."

"Yes, I think so too. Did you notice if there was anyone who didn't come down for breakfast this morning?"

"No, I didn't pay any attention. As it is, even on a regular workday we're spread out at several different tables at the back of the dining room and I suspect I wouldn't know if anyone was missing. But on Sundays, people tend to sleep in and trickle down to the dining room in dribs and drabs as long as they keep serving breakfast."

"Still," Geoffrey insisted, "it might help if we made a list of who you saw there—it would at least help us eliminate some of the potential suspects." He reached over, opened the glove compartment, and extracted a pad and pen which he handed to her. Hélissenne closed her eyes for a few moments to help her picture the scene, and jotted down a few names. She closed them again to try to picture the other tables near hers, and then to recall whom she had spoken with that morning in the dining room.

Her driver remained silent throughout her mental exercise, only speaking once she had finished writing. He asked her to read the list to him, even though he did not know everyone she worked with but only those she had mentioned either to say she liked them or to vent about them.

Two things stood out to him as she finished reading: she had made no mention of the site director, nor were any of the interns from English-speaking countries on her list. When he pointed this out to her, she explained—after getting over her surprise that Geoffrey might think Picard a shady enough character to do such a thing—that the site director generally sat at a table by himself at the other end of the dining room, almost never fraternizing with any of the students. She probably wouldn't have noticed him even if he had been there.

The American listened attentively as she shared her dim recollection that Picard had recently mentioned something about a box in her presence, noting that she dismissed its importance with the comment that she could remember neither when it had been nor in what context it had come up. She immediately added that she *had* in fact spotted Robert the Scotsman and Anne from Wales talking together at an adjoining table, but that it was true that she had not seen any of the Americans or English.

"What are their names?" Geoffrey inquired, as he pulled the car into the diminutive parking lot across from his hotel.

Hélissenne reflected for a moment. "Larry, Sarah, Randolph, Elizabeth …," she enunciated their names slowly and gropingly, as if looking around the archeological site to spot each of them in turn. "Also, I forgot—"

"You know, I noticed that guy Randolph at the café yesterday," Geoffrey cut in. "We were sitting outside, but I saw him at a table just inside the main door at some point, maybe before you got there. I've never liked the look of that guy," he added.

"That's just because you go to rival schools," Hélissenne ribbed him. "He's at Harvard, you're at Yale, and the hereditary feud between the schools lives on in you. I find him rather good-looking, even if he is incredibly full of himself."

"He certainly is full of himself," Geoffrey added peevishly, as they got out of the car, irked to hear any man but himself called good-looking. "Pretends to be God's gift to classics when he can't speak a word of Latin."

"Maybe, like most people, he understands it better than he speaks it."

"You mean he might have overheard us discussing your potential find?" Geoffrey wondered aloud, considering the possibility. "Now that I think of it, he was joined at his table by a couple of other people just before you arrived."

"Did you recognize them?"

"I think you once pointed them out to me as from Cambridge. I don't recall their names."

"You never do," Hélissenne commented flippantly, having noticed on many occasions Geoffrey's inability to recall people's names, even when he was introduced to them just moments before. "It was probably Bernard—he and Randolph seem to have become friends lately."

"Yes, I think it *was* him. There was a girl with Bernard, too."

"That must have been his fiancée, Allison. She's been visiting Bernard from England for the past week or so. Seems very nice." As they entered the hotel, Hélissenne added, "Come to think of it, I don't believe I saw them at breakfast this morning either."

VII

Geoffrey and Hélissenne ensconced themselves at the largest table in the main dining room and began to examine the oldest packet of letters first. Geoffrey had initially proposed that they read outside, since it was a fine day, but Hélissenne had pointed out that the wind might wreak havoc with the fragile parchment. The hotel's breakfast service had just ended, so they knew they would have a couple of quiet hours before them until the staff began to prepare the area for lunch.

The parchment was exceedingly old and brittle and the ink was terribly faded. Even Hélissenne, who was far more experienced in deciphering old Latin handwriting than her consort, seemed to be having a difficult time of it, despite the good lighting conditions right next to the window and the magnifying glass the American had brought down from his room.

Constitutionally far more impatient than she was, Geoffrey soon unwrapped the second packet of letters and was pleased to be able to read in a highly legible hand the very same lines on the first page of the new packet as Hélissenne had just managed to painstakingly decipher on the first page of the older packet. And comparing the last page of each of the packets, Hélissenne and Geoffrey were excited to find identical closing lines, followed on the newer paper by the laconic inscription in French: "Copied this last week of January 1543, M-d-M, M.d.N." Neither the date nor the complicated initials had any resonance whatsoever for Geoffrey, but they set off a subterranean train of thought in Hélissenne's mind. The lovers agreed to compare the two documents closely at some later point, sticking with the far more accessible version for the time being.

It quickly became clear that what they had before them was a set of intimate letters—there appeared to be well over a hundred of them in all at first glance—between a man and a woman. Their already considerable interest heightened as they noticed the obvious differences between the woman's way of addressing her lover and his way of addressing her.

After explaining the conventions of written greetings in medieval times to Geoffrey, Hélissenne pointed out to him that whereas in her first letter to her lover, the woman sends him her sincere wishes for "the freshness of eternal happiness," he, through the agency of the letter, sends her *himself*.

"A bit on the selfish side, don't you think?" she commented, looking at Geoffrey awry.

"I'd say it simply reflects his enthusiasm to be with her," objected Geoffrey. "After all, he sends himself to her in body and soul, as if he could not bear to be separated from her. I admit though," he added after rereading the first two short letters, "that whereas she sings his praises quite directly, he seems to bring everything back to himself, referring to her as the 'only solace of a weary mind,' indicating that his life without her is death."

"Yes, somehow it's all about him even when he's ostensibly complimenting her." Reading on a bit further, Hélissenne added, "Love for him seems to be a way to lose himself in her, to forget about his ambitions and intellectual preoccupations. Thinking about her, being with her, and writing to her seems to be a form of respite for him, a form of consolation for his difficulties and sufferings."

After these initial exchanges, which gave Geoffrey pause for thought, echoing as they did his own nocturnal ruminations, the two lovers fell silent as they became totally absorbed in their reading. It was only after they had finished perusing the entire collection of letters and had headed off into the nearby mountains for a hike that they discussed them further.

VIII

"I was struck by the fact," Geoffrey began, as they reached the first switchback, "that, if, as you said last night, the letters were likely written before the thirteenth century, the woman seems to see no contradiction whatsoever between carnal love and spiritual love for her partner. I thought everyone at that time believed the body to be corrupt and its passions degrading and unacceptable to God. And yet this woman proudly proclaims her attachment to her beloved as one involving her body, heart, mind, and soul, even calling him 'sweet medicine' for her body!"

"Yes," Hélissenne remarked somewhat dreamily, despite the steepness of the initial part of their climb into the densely wooded hills, "she strikes me as rather Old Testament in her views, citing passages from the *Song of Songs* celebrating lovers' unabashed enjoyment of each other. Worshipping her beloved's body is like worshipping God to her, since it is God's vessel."

"Wouldn't it have been considered rather heretical for someone to celebrate the body and its pleasures at that time?"

"I noticed that she always supports her views with biblical references, alluding in one instance to the passage, 'Your breasts are more beautiful than wine and the fragrance of your perfumes above all spices.'" Hélissenne blushed slightly as she said this, but Geoffrey, who was walking behind her, could not see her cheeks mantle. "But it's true—some of the things she says *might* have been considered rather daring. That's probably why they never mention the name of the person they are writing to in any of their letters. Prudence above all."

"Perhaps, too, they were not supposed to be writing to each other in the first place. At the outset I thought they might be cheating on their spouses with each other, or in some sort of courtly love situation, he courting a married noblewoman. But later on it seemed clear he was her teacher and that she believed him to be of higher station than herself."

"A belief he contests in one of his letters to her, after which she once perfunctorily says she is writing to him as an equal to an equal. It was unclear to me if he truly thought her to be of the same social class as himself or merely wished to raise her up in his own eyes to make her seem like an object worthy of his affection."

"I got the sense," objected Geoffrey, who was puffing pretty heavily due to the steep slope, "that he was highly impressed by her knowledge of classical letters, and thought that even Ovid and Cicero could have learned a thing or two from her about love and friendship."

"I never felt, though, that she was terribly pleased by such flattering words," Hélissenne reflected, panting rather less heavily than Geoffrey, her daily hikes up to her worksite having whipped her city-self into shape. "Even though she refers to a wealth of religious and literary texts, she strikes me as very modest about her knowledge and abilities and does not seem to want to be loved for her accomplishments or command of ancient languages."

"What *did* she seem to you to want to be loved for?"

Hélissenne thought about this for some moments. "I don't know. But I don't think a woman ever really wants to be loved for her accomplishments or mastery. Maybe it's different with

40

men," she added, looking up from the trail at Geoffrey, "but a woman wants to be loved for herself, not for something she has done."

At this, Geoffrey spun around to return her gaze. "The real question then is," he declared, "what is herself? What is this precious self she wants to be loved for?"

Hélissenne regarded Geoffrey rapturously, impressed by the profundity of the question. She reflected as they paused to enjoy the view of the village of Gincla that they now dominated by several hundred vertical feet.

"I guess it's easier to say what one doesn't want to be loved for than what one does," she confessed. "I wouldn't want to be loved just for my face, even though I would want it to be admired, or for my body, even though I would want it to be cherished. Nor would I want to be loved for my ability to cook or to read Latin, for I might end up feeling used by someone who esteemed me merely for those things."

Geoffrey tried to prod her to take this a step further, "So you would want to be loved for …?"

"For something else, for something almost impossible to describe. But I think it has to be something that makes me *different* from other people, not *like* everybody else. As our female letter writer put it, when it comes to love, it's not about being a neighbor or fellow man like everyone else who is deserving of care due to their generic humanity. Love for one's neighbor is the stuff of Christian charity, not of *dilectio*, not of my special love for you, for example." She took his hand passionately in hers and pressed it to her breast.

Geoffrey looked at her expectantly. "Tell me about this special love you have for me."

"Well," Hélissenne began quite seriously, "it's not about your good looks, your square jaw, your full head of hair, your cute accent—"

"You think my accent is cute?" Geoffrey inquired, smiling and drawing her toward him.

"Yes, I do," she replied, noticing that despite his request to know about her particular love for him, he took the first opportunity to keep the discussion on the lighter side.

"Well, if it is none of those things, it must be that you are enamored of my being such a successful Yalie."

Dismayed to hear him make such an unromantic comment, she rolled her eyes. "A woman might be impressed by a man's status or power," she demurred. "It might even excite her. But that's not what she loves—not if she truly loves."

"So my status excites you?" Geoffrey inquired, flying off on a tangent that preoccupied him not a little.

"I suppose it might if I were a naive American impressed by Ivy League colleges," she retorted, piqued at his apparent lack of interest in the topic of love. "As a French girl, however, …," she trailed off. "Anyway," she resumed, "being impressed or excited is not the same as loving."

"So what is it you love about me?" Geoffrey asked, with mock seriousness. "My fabulous personality? My chivalrous manners? My scintillating intellect?"

"Hardly!" To punish him for changing the subject, she pretended to think very carefully and come up with nothing whatsoever, in the end shrugging her shoulders as he held her with both arms around her waist.

He raised his eyebrows at her, as if cut to the quick.

"I guess it's your soul I love," she conceded, taking things seriously again. "Your spirit."

"Good save," he thought to himself. Then aloud, he said, "Luckily for you, the soul is virtually impossible to describe."

Hélissenne smiled uneasily at this, and as they set off again up the mountain trail toward the 4000-foot summit of the Pech des Carabatets, she wondered to herself about the relationship between love and the concept of the soul in religion. In a more worldly vein, her companion wondered to himself—as if for the very first time—what a woman might possibly find to love in him.

Having trod in silence for a few pensive minutes, Hélissenne, whose musings had eventually turned to other matters, reflected aloud, "It seems to me that the female letter writer views her learning as a means for getting close to her beloved, and perhaps even as a salve for his absence, since she often complains of him staying away too long. Studying the classical authors was maybe a way for her to feel close to him when he was far away."

"Is that the way it is for you with me?" inquired Geoffrey, tongue-in-cheek, stopping in the middle of the trail, wrapping his arms around Hélissenne's waist again, and pulling her close to him. "You dive back into your musty medieval manuscripts when I am not available in order to feel closer to me?"

"You found me out," she said, kissing him quickly on the lips. "Except that you're always available."

Geoffrey contrived indignation. "What about my weekday mornings, when I engage in activities of which you are completely unaware?"

"Unaware? Come on," Hélissenne exclaimed, laughing. "You give me a thorough accounting every afternoon of your morning activities. In fact you tell me your every waking thought and deed."

"Well," Geoffrey protested, looking past her down to the town of Salvezines that had just come into view, "if you believe those stories ..."

"Shouldn't I?"

"You never know with men."

"You mean they aren't trustworthy?"

"Some men lead double lives."

"You might be having an affair with Madame Cochenille, your hotelier?" she asked, smiling. The surprised look on Geoffrey's face was enough to indicate that he had never even so much as entertained the idea of forming a dalliance with the rather attractive but cantankerous hotel owner. But Hélissenne went on with her joking, "You might be one of those guys one reads about in magazines who assiduously court one woman, all the while having sex with another? One of those boys my girlfriends tell me about who act as if love and sex were incompatible?"

Geoffrey was taken aback by the turn the conversation had taken. He brushed off the not-quite-serious questions with a laugh and quickly asked Hélissenne if she had gotten the sense that the relationship between the man and woman who wrote the letters had become physical at some point.

Hardly oblivious to the abrupt change in subject, she nonetheless replied to his question in the affirmative and added that she had in fact gotten the sense that the man in the exchange had become angry with the woman after they began being intimate, as if he—unlike her—felt guilty about their carnal relations, as if he felt they had committed some kind of crime.

"Reading between the lines," she added, "I almost got the sense he was angry with himself for giving into the passions of the flesh, and for getting so caught up in them that he was neglecting his teaching, work he considered to be much more important than love and sex. I had the distinct impression he was taking out his anger at himself on her, saying mean things to her, and treating her badly."

Geoffrey released her waist during this last exchange and pretended to be absorbed in looking at the sublime scenery. Puilaurens Castle was directly across the valley from them now, although its proud battlements were barely visible, cloaked as they were in mist.

"Given that they were both obviously Catholic," Hélissenne went on after a short while, "she should have reminded him that if the heart is pure, what the body does cannot be sinful. As it is, she accuses him of having borne the pleasure of 'desired joy' as if he were angry."

They strode up the trail in silence for a little while again, the American fighting a certain sinking feeling.

"I think that was the point in their correspondence," the Poitevine reflected, "when she called the whole thing off and insisted he stop writing to her."

"So you thought *that* was why she got so annoyed with him?" queried Geoffrey, thankful for an opportunity to change the subject. "I thought maybe he suspected she had inadvertently revealed something about their relations to someone—"

"That's possible, of course."

"—when he himself had perhaps slipped up, having left a tablet around where indiscrete eyes might have read it or having spoken too openly of their trysts," he hastened to finish his sentence. "People do tend," he added, giving her a meaningful look, "to accuse their nearest and dearest of the very things they themselves are guilty of or have done wrong."

IX

Hélissenne stopped, rooted to the spot.

Geoffrey's comment had brought back to mind something she had read in recent months. It involved a man saying he suspected a woman of merely pretending when she claimed not to be seeking praise. It was not Jane Austen's Darcy, although he had once said much the same thing. No, the author she was thinking of had likened the woman in question to the nymph Galatea, described by Virgil as running to hide in the willows, all the while wanting to be seen.

It suddenly dawned on her that the author was Peter Abelard, the twelfth-century philosopher who taught at the Notre-Dame Cathedral School in Paris and was castrated owing to his intimate relations with Heloise, a beautiful and well-educated student whose so-called honor was being jealously guarded by a brutish uncle. When she had read the letters Heloise and Abelard had exchanged many years after their intimate relations had ceased, he then being in a monastery and she in a convent, Hélissenne had observed that Abelard criticized Heloise for praise-seeking whereas his whole life up until then might have been seen as one enormous search for fame and glory!

When she mentioned this to Geoffrey, who asked why she had suddenly halted smack in the middle of the trail, he indicated that he was familiar with the fateful story of Abelard and Heloise's love. He reminded her of two points in the letters they had just read at which the man accuses the woman of actively looking for opportunities to sever their relationship, whereas the overall tenor of her letters suggests no interest whatsoever on her part in creating a rift between them. Perhaps, he speculated, Abelard was the one who was looking for an opportunity to put an end to their relationship, owing to qualms he had about the physical intimacy between them, but blamed *her* for doing so. "Talk about the pot calling the kettle black," the American couldn't stop himself from exclaiming aloud in English, even though he knew Hélissenne would have no idea what it meant.

But, in any case, Hélissenne wasn't listening. It had suddenly struck her that Heloise and Abelard, the infamous letter writers of around 1130, were known to have sent numerous letters to each other when their love affair first began some sixteen years earlier. She recalled hearing that there was heated debate over a series of letters that had recently been discovered in an archive in France, some scholars claiming that they were very likely excerpts from the early letters exchanged between Heloise and Abelard.

"It might well be the same author who used the same rhetorical strategy in the two cases," Hélissenne cried excitedly. She quickly filled Geoffrey in on the controversy surrounding the abridged letters found in 1974 in the library in the town of Troyes.

They had been selectively transcribed by a well-respected monk in the fifteenth century, Jean de la Véprie—or Johannes de Vepria, as she told Geoffrey—who was particularly interested in the creative salutations and leave-takings found in their opening and closing lines. None of the letters had contained any names or dates and thus couldn't definitively be attributed to any particular authors, but a certain medievalist had pretty convincingly shown that they must have been Abelard and Heloise.

"What we found," she bubbled over, "might well be the original letters that no one has ever before seen—well, no one except Jean de la Véprie and perhaps a few of his friends in the late fourteen hundreds!"

Hélissenne's excitement was infectious and Geoffrey immediately proposed that, instead of going on to the nearby summit, they return to the hotel so he could run a search for the Latin text in the giant Yale classics database he had access to as a graduate student. On the way back down the trail, he prattled enthusiastically about their publishing an unexpurgated edition of these long-lost love letters, with Hélissenne providing a translation of them into French, and him writing an introduction. He proposed to research all the references to classical texts in the letters, of which he was already sure there were plenty, having recognized snatches of Horace, Juvenal, and Cicero here and there.

"And then," he went on precipitately, "after I bone up on my medieval Latin, I'll prepare an English translation and *you* can write the introduction."

Mindful of the unstinting labor such grand plans would entail, she admired his eagerness and kept to herself the reflection that the documents were hardly theirs to do with as they pleased.

X

Geoffrey came galloping down the hotel stairs cursing in what to Hélissenne's ears seemed to be English, though unlike any she had learned in school. The Poitevine was at one of the tables on the terrace, sitting near a number of hotel guests having late-afternoon tea or an apéritif, waiting for her beloved to bring down his laptop so they could check the letters they had found against the tens of thousands of classical texts included in the Yale library database. He gestured to her impatiently to join him in the reception area where the svelte and carefully coiffed hotelier, Madame Cochenille, was working.

No sooner was Hélissenne in earshot of ordinary volume speech than her beloved exclaimed, "Now *my* room has been ransacked! Somebody obviously really wants those letters and wasn't after your fake Cartier."

The Poitevine reeled slightly and Geoffrey steadied her by guiding her by the elbow toward the reception desk, against which they both leaned.

"I guess it wasn't so ridiculous after all to ask Madame Cochenille to put the letters in her safe while we went out hiking," Geoffrey continued, but there was no bitterness in his voice at the recollection that Hélissenne had thought it superfluous when he had initially mentioned it. "We'd better tell her someone's rifled through my stuff."

Mme. Cochenille, whose English was rather more serviceable than Hélissenne's, responded to Geoffrey's story in her habitually undiplomatic way. "That's impossible," she pronounced with end-of-story finality.

It didn't matter that she had known Geoffrey for six weeks already and grown to appreciate him as a serious, levelheaded young man. *Anyone* who said *anything* that contradicted her idyllic view of her establishment was obviously mistaken and guilty of *lèse-majesté*.

"No one could have been able to go into your room," she added, putting another nail in the coffin of his assertion.

Geoffrey, who had heard the hotel owner make similar proclamations to himself and to numerous other guests as well—to the effect that it could not possibly have been too hot or too cold in someone's room, that there could not possibly have been too many mosquitoes—patiently explained that the lock on his door had been forced and the entire room turned upside down.

The hotelier, who was not closed to all instruction—assuming one took the time and care to handle her properly, assuring her, whether it were true or not, that whatever was wrong had occurred through no fault of her own—then became pensive. She informed Geoffrey that he had had a visitor while out hiking, someone who claimed to be an American friend of his. Seeing the confused expression on Geoffrey's face, Mme. Cochenille described this alleged friend as towheaded, about six feet tall, and with a not-too-pronounced American accent adorning his fairly good French.

When Geoffrey indicated that he didn't have any American friends in the area, and that his friends didn't even know where he was, Mme. Cochenille expressed relief that she hadn't shown this man the letters in the safe.

52

"The letters in the safe?" cried Geoffrey. "He knew about the letters and that they were in the safe?"

"Not precisely," she replied, looking away momentarily. "Certainly, he knew something about the letters. He mentioned that the two of you worked together in classics, deciphering ancient documents, and casually mentioned letters in the course of the conversation. I am sorry it may be my fault he learned the letters are in the safe," she continued, "because my eyes naturally looked toward the safe when he mentioned letters. I was truly shocked when he had the nerve to ask if he could see them."

All of Geoffrey's features registered worry and he spoke a few quick words to Hélissenne to ensure that she had understood the gist of their conversation. Turning back to speak to Mme. Cochenille, he stated that he knew full well she was under no obligation whatsoever to comply with his request, but entreated her nevertheless not to open the safe for anyone except himself and Hélissenne.

Geoffrey had made the proper offering on the altar of the hotelier's dignity. Like so many other French service providers, any request that she was not required by law or by written agreement to accede to was met with an immediate "No," uttered automatically out of principle. But once the general point that she was in no way *required* to grant the petitioner's wishes had been accepted—in other words, once her initial refusal had been acquiesced to by the hotel guest or restaurant diner—there was no telling how magnanimous and munificent her "Yes" might be, how far out of her way she might go to graciously serve the public to whom she *owed* nothing. Her generosity and benevolence had to be utterly and completely gratuitous, not commanded.

Geoffrey had exculpated her staff by explaining that the lock to the door of his room had been forced, and he had assured her that he knew full well he was asking for something he had no right to expect. Were that not sufficient, Mme. Cochenille felt just the slightest bit guilty that she had unwittingly revealed the location of the letters ...

"I assure you that I will open the safe only for the two of you," Mme. Cochenille replied simply.

"That's a load off my mind," Geoffrey said, heaving a sigh of relief.

"I must say," Mme. Cochenille began anew, "that there was something about this American that made me uncomfortable. When I told him that I could not show him anything you had not personally agreed to let him see, he made some curious hand gestures and eye gestures, peering at me intently as if he wanted to throw me a spell or entrance me."

"Oh my God," exclaimed Geoffrey. "He is probably an amateur hypnotist of some kind. I see that we're up against somebody who has more than one trick up his sleeve."

"I think there must be at least two persons," the hotel owner interjected. "I saw this alleged friend of yours arrive and depart, and there was no moment where he could have climbed up to your room and ransacked it without me noticing."

XI

G eoffrey and Hélissenne became intoxicated by the fine food and drink they treated themselves to at the hotel restaurant that night, having confirmed that the letters were indeed a complete version of those reputed to be the early love letters between Abelard and Heloise. The awestruck students toasted and re-toasted their luck at having made such an incredible find.

The late August mountain air was pure and balmy, the Milky Way sparkled brightly across the entire sky despite the dazzling moonlight, and the lovers ambled languorously around the village after dessert, so tightly intertwined that they seemed to be one not two. So often did they stop to embrace each other still more closely, the tiny village allowed them a lengthy stroll.

Unable to get enough of each other, they turned their steps toward the village anew whenever they approached the hotel, endlessly deferring the moment of parting, disagreeing with Shakespeare as to the sweetness of its sorrow.

It was only as Geoffrey drove Hélissenne back to her hotel after midnight that their earlier concerns forced their way back into consciousness. Two attempts to appropriate the letters had been made that day, and they had yet to decide when and how to bring the letters to the attention of the director of the dig. Still they reckoned that the documents were in good hands now and that they would come up with a sensible plan that would both give them credit for the find and return the documents to their rightful owner, whoever that might be.

Even though passages of the letters occasionally crossed Geoffrey's mind during the drive, he could only really focus on two things: the importance of the publication that would be likely to issue from their discovery, and their tenacious rival—or rather rivals. It occurred to him as they arrived at Hélissenne's hotel that the breaking and entering of his room must have been an inside job, since the hotel owner had not seen anyone except registered guests enter or leave the premises all day.

"I have to remember to ask Madame Cochenille if anyone new checked in today as soon as I get back tonight," Geoffrey commented.

"Yes, once they realized that what they were after was not in my room, they must have figured it was in yours. No doubt they thought they would have an easier time searching your room if they were hotel guests themselves than if they tried to sneak in from the outside."

"And right they were. They probably watched us leave the hotel in our hiking boots and figured the time was ripe," he reasoned, as he exited the car and came around to open the door for her. "We may well not have heard the last of them yet," Geoffrey cautioned her. "We shall have to be especially vigilant. You promise you will be, *carissima*?" he demanded firmly, folding her in his arms.

"I promise. *Vale, omnis dilectio mea*," she replied, giving her love an ardent kiss goodnight.

XII

When Geoffrey entered the courtyard of Puilaurens Castle a mere twelve hours later, Hélissenne was nowhere to be found. After asking a few of the interns if they had seen her that day, he sought out Hélissenne's best friend, Isabeau, and asked her.

She was an attractive, redheaded Breton, whose spoken Latin was not nearly as developed as Hélissenne's, but whose colloquial English was pretty good. "When I did not see her at breakfast this morning or in the van on the way to work, I assumed she was with you," Isabeau said, pausing knowingly, "in your hotel."

Isabeau had been jealous of Hélissenne throughout the second half of the summer, having found Geoffrey far and away more handsome and interesting than any of the male interns or local yokels she had come across in their little corner of southwestern France. She had initially been attracted to Bernard from Cambridge who, although not bad looking and a rather sweet little lambkin who had done her and Hélissenne a few signal favors, turned out to be already spoken for. At any rate, he would have been no more than a convenient summer boy toy for her. She had then found herself taken with Randolph's status and wealth. She had flirted with the

Harvard student a bit early on in the summer, but eventually found him too whiny and pretentious for her taste. Her boyfriend back in Poitiers continued to write her impassioned e-mail, to whatever degree e-mail allows for the conveyance of fervor, but she was bored with him, finding Hélissenne's American far more delectable. Whether she would have found him so very fantabulous had Hélissenne not manifested a clear preference for him, she couldn't say for sure, having long since realized she often had a thing for guys her closest friends were involved with.

Not at all indignant at Isabeau's implication that Hélissenne had been with him since the day before at his hotel, Geoffrey explained, "But she wasn't—I dropped her off at your hotel around twelve-thirty last night."

"Maybe she is making the fat morning," she remarked. Seeing the uncomprehending look on Geoffrey's face, she added, "You know, sleeping more than usual. We girls sometimes do that sort of thing," she added, disporting herself by giving her long red locks and shoulders a sensual shake, as though she herself were just waking up, and wishing to remind Geoffrey that Hélissenne was not the only girl on God's great earth.

"Maybe, but I think it could be a lot more serious than that."

"Serious?" Isabeau asked, trying to imagine what the problem could be. "In what way?"

Receiving no answer from him, but seeing his grim countenance, Isabeau figured this was no joke and packed up her things and immediately went in search of Hélissenne with him.

There was no response when they knocked at their friend's room at the hotel and no one at the front desk or in the dining room had the slightest idea what had become of her. Isabeau and Geoffrey checked all the common areas at the hotel thoroughly, and then examined her room top to bottom thanks to a maid who knew Isabeau and opened the door for her. Hélissenne's bed had not been slept in!

They visited the few shops and cafés she might have gone to, but to no avail. Finally, Geoffrey implored Isabeau to accompany him to the local police station to file a missing person report. She conveyed his worries to the police, but they essentially laughed at him, intimating that the American's girlfriend had probably just gone off with another guy and would come back to him when she tired of her newfound paramour.

Isabeau chose not to translate the entirety of her conversation with the gendarmes into English for Geoffrey, but he got the general picture when he saw one of the officers hold up his index finger and pinky behind his head as if they were horns and heard the generally riotous guffaws among the policemen. His blood began to boil at this insinuation and he gave vent to his indignation in English, surprising all present. This seemed to silence the assembly, and the officer in charge eventually indicated to Isabeau that if Hélissenne were still missing in a couple of days, they would issue an alert.

XIII

"Do you have any pictures of Hélissenne that I could show around?" Geoffrey asked Isabeau as they left the police station.

"What do you mean?"

"Close-ups or good quality pictures that I could show to the hotel staff and local merchants to ask if any of them have seen her today. Just because the police won't initiate an inquiry doesn't mean I won't explore every avenue."

Isabeau opened her backpack, located her wallet, and began to check for any pictures of Hélissenne she might have on her. Coming up empty-handed, she remarked, "But I'm sure I have some pictures you could use in my room. Let's go back to the hotel." There was nothing in any way suggestive in this last remark, Isabeau having concluded that—although a little flirtation now and then between friends, especially when relationships had yet to be set in stone, was fair play—the situation was grave and she needed to put that sort of thing aside. She proposed that they solicit the assistance of Bernard, who had proved so helpful on a couple of other occasions, and his fiancée, Allison, who, although Isabel was loath to admit it as she had been an unknown rival for Bernard's affections at the beginning of the summer, seemed friendly enough. Allison would almost certainly be available, since she was there on vacation, not for work.

Isabeau and Geoffrey turned their footsteps toward their new destination and Geoffrey set a very fast pace. "I'd heard that the police in this country were remarkably unconcerned about theft," he commented after they had gone a few blocks, "but you'd think they believed you could just contact your insurance company to get your beloved replaced with another as if she were a stolen piece of jewelry. Unbelievable," he exclaimed.

"She is irreplaceable to you?" inquired Isabeau, who was struggling to walk as fast as Geoffrey. "Is that how you feel about her already?"

"Already? I've felt like that about her since the very first day I met her! The feeling has simply grown stronger with every passing moment."

"Really?" Isabeau queried, stopping their forced march to the hotel as she scrutinized his face closely.

"You don't believe me?" Geoffrey asked incredulously, coming to a complete stop too. "Has Hélissenne told you something I don't know—does she think I'm simply playing games with her?" He, in turn, examined the Frenchwoman's face closely.

"No, it's nothing like that. It's just that Hélissenne is my best friend and I worry about her. She doesn't take things lightly like I do, and getting involved with a foreigner who is probably planning on returning to the United States in a couple of weeks after a midsummer fling in—"

"Is that how you see my relationship with Hélissenne?" Geoffrey cut in indignantly. "I thought you knew me better than that by now."

"I know that you are very taken with her for the instant," Isabeau replied calmly, "but I worry that you mean more to Hélissenne than she does to you."

"She told you I mean a lot to her?"

"I didn't say that," Isabeau replied, playing her cards carefully, not wanting to betray Hélissenne's confidence. "It's just my impression that …"

"That?" Geoffrey prodded her to go on as she weighed her words.

"That she would be very hurt if you left just like that."

"Well, you can rest assured that I have absolutely no intention of leaving."

"But aren't you returning to the faculty soon?" she asked, looking him square in the eye. "Won't classes be starting again shortly?"

At this, Geoffrey looked down, avoiding Isabeau's gaze. "They *will* be starting again soon. I've been planning on … well, I've been toying with the idea of taking a year off and following Hélissenne to Poitiers."

He raised his head and his eyes met Isabeau's. "What exactly does this expression of yours mean—toying with?" she asked pointedly, now siding decidedly with Hélissenne.

Without being fully cognizant of it, Isabeau had put her finger on a sore point, but Geoffrey did his best to suppress any suspicion he himself had occasionally had that he was merely toying with Hélissenne's feelings. "It means that I am trying to work out the details—I have to request a leave of absence and find some way of supporting myself for the coming year."

"I'm relieved to hear it," Isabeau said, even though she did not entirely trust the explanation Geoffrey had provided of the idiomatic expression he had spontaneously employed and made a mental note to look it up later.

Hélissenne's friends proceeded anew to the hotel and, after picking up a couple of good likenesses of her that highlighted her thick waist-length hair and slender frame, spent the remainder of the afternoon showing them to the hotel staff and local merchants, and even to some of the town's *pétanque* players who might just possibly have seen her walk by at some point during their endless matches. But no one had seen her, and when Bernard came back to town for dinner along with the other members of the archeological team, he confirmed that she had not made an appearance at the dig all day. He expressed his concern and immediately offered to do whatever he could to help them find her.

XIV

The mystery of Hélissenne's whereabouts was not solved when Geoffrey returned to his hotel, for no message or note from her awaited him. Yet he was convinced that she wouldn't of her own accord have gone anywhere for this long without telling him, even had there been an emergency of some kind, like a death in her family. He spent the night in an agitated state, but by morning had decided upon a course of action. Were there still no trace of Hélissenne at her hotel by now, Geoffrey would bring in professional help. A professor of his at Yale had once mentioned a sort of private detective she knew, someone who had apparently helped one of her good friends out of a jam. What seemed so perfect about this particular detective, if Geoffrey recalled correctly what the professor had told him, was that he was French.

The cost, he said to himself, might well be exorbitant, but cost be damned!

Upon returning to his hotel for lunch, having spent the morning showing her picture all around the town of Lapradelle once again, he perceived that a note had been slipped under his hotel room door. On the most banal typewriter paper imaginable, the kind that could be purchased in any stationery or grocery store in France, in the most generic Times Roman laser printer-generated font, was a terse proposition in English to switch the find for the girl:

> We know what you have and you know what we have.
> The exchange will occur at the Cabane de la Balmette on Friday at noon.
> Come alone or else!

Shuddering at the likely implications of the note for Hélissenne, and realizing for the first time that the people they were up against would stop at nothing to get what they wanted—hardly the sort of scholarly rivals he had imagined—Geoffrey searched for the designated location on his map of the Pyrenees. It was both at a considerable distance from Gincla and appeared to be accessible only on foot, and that after a ten-mile hike into what showed every indication of being rugged backcountry. The physical effort was nothing to him as compared to the fact that he would have no guarantee that Hélissenne would actually be there when he arrived or that they would release her as promised, there being so little honor among thieves. Moreover, he reflected, her abductors would be able to do with him as they pleased, he being easy prey for them in such a remote location. How would he be able to ensure that the exchange really occurred, assuming he was willing to give up the letters in the first place?

Could there be, Geoffrey wondered to himself, anything they might want other than the letters? Did they intend to relieve Hélissenne and him of their very lives? Hélissenne had no doubt seen their faces or at least heard their voices by now and could potentially testify against them. He himself might soon become an eyewitness, and the abductors would then have every reason to want to dispose of both of them.

Articles he had read in the papers about the white slave trade flitted through his mind, but he tried to push them aside. Unsuccessfully. Could anyone, he couldn't help but reflect, interested in such arcane love letters stoop so low as to sell someone into sexual slavery? How could anyone with supposedly academic interests even imagine such a thing? But, then, hadn't he himself just imagined it? (What this said about him he did not pause to consider.)

It suddenly occurred to him that he had perhaps misjudged their assailants. The people who had overheard their conversation or seen them retrieve something from the castle dig might actually have no real idea what the couple had found but simply presumed it must be of great monetary value. Perhaps Geoffrey had been naively optimistic in thinking it was Randolph and his anglophone student buddies who had overheard them. There was, he knew, a species of opportunists known as treasure hunters—people who were far more interested in the exchange value than in the historical value of the artifacts they unearthed or brought up from the depths of the ocean. Perhaps he was not dealing with university types at all.

XV

Fuming inside because he had to wait until it was a decent hour in New Haven before moving forward, given the six-hour time difference between France and the East Coast, he finally called his professor after lunch—Geoffrey was never one to lose his appetite no matter how dire the circumstances or how ill he was—and obtained the number for a certain Inspector Canal. According to this teacher of his, the gentleman had reportedly retired from the French Secret Service and was now living in New York. Although she found him to be a quirky, touchy sort of fellow, he had a knack for getting the job done.

Anxious to get the ball rolling, Geoffrey was crestfallen when Ferguson, the man with a British accent who answered the phone at Canal's number, informed him that the inspector was away on vacation. Detecting a sense of urgency in Geoffrey's voice and in those details of his predicament that the American was willing to convey to him when he inquired as to the purport of his call, Ferguson promised to get in touch with Canal who would in turn contact Geoffrey shortly. Canal's valet remained a model of politeness as he nevertheless refused Geoffrey's repeated requests for some phone number at which he could contact Canal directly himself.

Geoffrey almost lost his temper at this stonewalling, but Ferguson firmly assured him that he would phone Canal immediately and that Geoffrey would hear from the inspector within a couple of hours at the very most.

Somewhat mollified outwardly, but still burning up inside, Geoffrey sat at the desk in his hotel room, glaring at the telephone. Indulging in harsh thoughts about an inspector who had the effrontery to go away on vacation in August, Geoffrey failed to notice that the phone in his room had begun ringing, he only picking it up after the fourth ring.

An unprepared Geoffrey muttered into the phone, "Hello? I mean, *Allô, oui*?"

"Is zis Geoffrey Whitman?" a deep male voice asked, with an unmistakable French accent.

Geoffrey came to himself, "Yes it is. Who's calling?"

"No, ze name is Canal, not Hooze," the Frenchman replied to see if the American had any sense of humor.

If he did, he didn't show it now. "Oh, Inspector Canal, thank you for calling so quickly."

"No problem. Ferguson made it sound rather urgent, so I thought it best to call right away."

"Ferguson?"

"Yes, the man you spoke with on the phone earlier. What made you call me? Not many people know of me."

"I am a student of Professor Bellman's at Yale, and she told me about your work on a purloined something or other."

Canal was perplexed and even a bit embarrassed, wondering how Bellman could have known about his early opus on Edgar Allan Poe published under a pseudonym. He even sheepishly recalled having once failed to show up for a speaking engagement he had accepted at the venerable university, rather impolitely as a matter of fact, the people who had invited him thinking it scandalous and not extending a new invitation for ten whole years. The only word he uttered was, "Yes?"

"I think it was some sort of purloined liqueur—what was it called? That green stuff, Chartreuse."

"*Ah, oui,*" Canal exhaled, reassured.

"Yes, I believe Professor Bellman is a friend of the woman you helped with that liqueur, if I got the details right."

"*Oui, ça doit être cela,*" Canal said to himself. "I see," he said aloud, recalling his enjoyable adventures with Sandra Errand. "My man Ferguson told me your lady love has been abducted because someone is trying to come into the possession of a collection of old intimate letters you found at Puilaurens."

"Yes, that's right," the Midwesterner replied, even if the syntagm *lady love* struck him as oddly old-fashioned.

"They would not have anything to do with ze lost love letters of Heloise and Abelard, now would they?" Canal inquired offhandedly.

Geoffrey was stunned and could utter not a syllable.

"Your silence speaks volumes. But rest assured, there is no extrasensory perception involved here. I was just hoping that someday the complete letters might come to light, and I see that my wish has been fulfilled," remarked the inspector, who saw to it that his desires often became realities. "You still have the letters in your possession?"

"I do, but I may not be able to keep them for very much longer—I just received a note from the kidnappers demanding the letters in exchange for my girlfriend."

"And you do not want to hand them over?"

"Not if I don't have to. They constitute a very important find."

"Can you describe this girl to me?"

Geoffrey was rather nonplussed. "What good would that do you?"

"So I could recognize her, just in case I run into her on my way to see you," Canal replied, as if it were the most natural thing in the world.

71

"You mean you're willing to take on the case?" Geoffrey inquired jubilantly.

"Between the inducements of a missing girl, long-lost love letters, and the fact that I had been planning to get out of the city and into the mountains for the past week anyway, how could I say no?"

"I'm afraid I don't have much money to pay for you to fly over here, or for a decent hotel, or for other expenses, or for your fees," Geoffrey proffered, the proliferation of details getting in the way of his apology.

"We will talk about all of that later. The fact is that I am already in France, staying at my pied-à-terre in L'Île Saint-Louis."

"Staying in Lille?" Geoffrey asked, not having understood the last part of Canal's statement. "Rue de Lille?"

For the second time in the course of his conversation with this American, Canal was taken aback. "Rue de Lille? What did this young man know about rue de Lille? *How* could he know about rue de Lille?" Aloud the inspector inquired, "What did you ask me?"

Geoffrey too was confused. "I wasn't sure if you said you were in the town of Lille or in Lille Street."

"Neither, I am in L'Île Saint-Louis, an island in the middle of Paris not far from Notre Dame. I can leave directly and should be able to make it to Gincla—that is where you are lodging, is it not?"

"Yes, that's right," Geoffrey replied with surprise in his voice that the Frenchman could divine where he was staying.

"I should be able to make it there by lunchtime tomorrow. Shall I meet you at your hotel?"

"That would be wonderful," Geoffrey gushed, pleased that reinforcements would be arriving so soon. He had figured that Canal would not be able to get a plane out of New York until the next day at the earliest, since it was high season, and that he would then have to take a second plane to Toulouse. In short, he had been suspecting that most of the seventy hours until the exchange at the Cabane de la Balmette would have elapsed before the inspector's arrival. "It's the Hostellerie du Grand Duc located—"

"Unless things have changed a great deal in the last few years," Canal cut in, "there is only one hotel in Gincla. I will not fail to find you."

"Right," Geoffrey conceded, standing corrected. "Is there anything I should do between now and then?"

"First, limn the girl for me so I can form a picture of her in my mind."

Although Geoffrey could not understand the point of this exercise, he did his best to comply with the request. "Hélissenne has very long chestnut-colored hair and is of about medium height—I don't know, somewhere between five foot three and five foot eight?"

Canal waited a few moments for Geoffrey to go on. When he didn't, the inspector inquired, "Is zat all? It does not give me much to go on."

"What else would you like to know?"

"What color are her eyes?"

"Let me see … They're brown." After glancing at one of the photographs he had of her in his room, he added, "No, they're more like green."

"You mean hazel?"

"I'm afraid I'm not very good with colors. I've never quite known what color hazel is."

"*Passons*," Canal muttered under his breath. "You will show me some pictures when I get there. Have the kidnappers already proposed a meeting time and place?"

"Yes, Friday at noon in a remote location in the Pyrenees, about a ten-mile hike up into the mountains, from what I can see on the map."

"Well, it does not give us a lot of time. So I would recommend you reconnoiter the location carefully to see what kind of terrain we will be working with and what kind of cover we will have, if any."

"Will do—I'll go this afternoon," Geoffrey replied, grateful to have something concrete to do with his nervous energy. "Anything else you'd like me to do?"

The Frenchman reflected for a moment and then replied, "All that it suffices to do is to book me a room—I will see you at lunch tomorrow."

XVI

Geoffrey was beside himself as he awaited Canal's arrival the next morning. He had been going over and over in his mind what he intended to tell the inspector since scouting out the remote meeting area in the mountains the afternoon and evening before, given that it had been a rocky, challenging climb leading to what looked to him like a dangerous, unforgiving location for an exchange of anything other than blood, sweat, and tears.

When the noon hour came and went, the American began first to fidget, then to jiggle his leg up and down under the table on the terrace at which he was keeping a lookout for the inspector, and finally to drum on the lunch table so loudly that several of the nearby diners gave him nasty looks. By twelve-thirty he began to think that Canal had had second thoughts and decided not to come, and by twelve-forty-five he had convinced himself the inspector had had a car accident and would never make it to Gincla at all.

But he was wrong. If Canal was going to have second thoughts, he generally had them right away and never promised anything he thought there might possibly be a chance he would be unable to deliver. Moreover, he was sure and steady at the wheel, ever the alert and defensive driver. He simply arrived at the hotel an hour later than Geoffrey expected him. To the American, lunch began precisely at noon, whereas to Canal one or so was a perfectly acceptable lunch hour, especially since he tended to be a late riser and breakfasted long after most New Yorkers had already left for work.

During the journey south from Paris, Canal had been turning over in his mind the various details of the story he had thus far been told. He understood Geoffrey's reluctance to hand over the letters, but wondered what his motives were to perhaps prefer them to the very girl he professed to love. Perhaps she was not nearly as important to him as he had made her out to be when he had spoken with Ferguson.

The vagueness of the description he had given of the girl contrasted sharply with depictions he had heard from infatuated men, even if their verbal descriptions of people's visual appearance were generally quite impoverished compared to those furnished by members of the fairer sex. Even Abelard, who rarely talked about Heloise's features, must have noticed the color of her eyes, since he raved, "My stars, should you ask, are two. I know no others: they are those starry eyes of yours. When I enjoy them, I feel that I am lacking for nothing, when I am denied them, that I am lacking for everything."

Canal was forced to wonder whether Geoffrey was not more attached to the letters than he was to Hélissenne. Perhaps, like certain readers, he had fallen in love with the Heloise of the letters and preferred her to the flesh and blood Hélissenne. Or was he attached to Hélissenne primarily *because* of the letters?

Canal was surprised that the American had called upon him instead of simply photographing all the letters, which would have provided him with a copy as well as proof of first possession, and then turning over the letters to the kidnappers in exchange for this allegedly precious girlfriend of his. There must be some sort of war raging in this boy's mind, he figured, to make him incapable of solving this seemingly straightforward problem. Well, he would get a glimpse of the dilemma whose horns the student was caught on soon enough, he told himself.

Upon greeting Geoffrey, the Frenchman explained that he had been unable to resist taking a short detour via one of his favorite villages, Curemonte, on the way down to Gincla. That was, after all, he explained, where he had intended to begin his vacation in the mountains prior to hearing from Ferguson that there was a new case in the offing. Geoffrey would have preferred that the inspector lie, and say he had run into bad traffic, rather than hear that the private detective he had just hired placed personal indulgence before professionalism in a matter of life and death.

This was hardly to be Geoffrey's last disappointment, however, for no sooner had Canal shaken his hand and seated himself at the table across from the graduate student, than he picked up the food and wine menus, contemplated them silently at some length, and then called the waitress over and ordered for the both of them a rather sumptuous sounding four-course meal, complete with an expensive Collioure wine.

Geoffrey, who had expected to lunch somewhat spartanly and get right down to brass tacks, was confused and communicated this to Canal as soon as the waitress had left them. Canal, who had his own ideas about how investigations ought to proceed, assured him that a wholesome meal would do them a lot more good than hours of cogitation and that an indirect approach often turned out to be more direct in the end than an ostensibly direct approach.

"Come again?" Geoffrey uttered.

Canal expressed his thoughts again in slightly different terms, though still pronouncing every *th* like *z* and every *is* like *ease*. "Zinking on an empty stomach ease often quite fruitless, in my experience. And what may appear at first glance to be an indirect route to one's destination often turns out to be more direct zan what had appeared at first glance to be a direct route."

"I see," Geoffrey replied, although it was not clear to him that he really did, even if he was willing to consider the possibility.

"The point is to go where the obstacles are not—in any case, not to be especially interested in obstacles," Canal concluded, quoting something he had once formulated in another context, finding it reasonably apt here. His interlocutor nodded politely.

A waiter came by with the *amuse-bouches*, mini-portions of a sort of cream of asparagus, and Geoffrey launched into a description of the rendezvous site that had been proposed by the kidnappers. "I did what you said yesterday, and checked out the site the abductors proposed for the exchange, the Cabane de la Balmette. It's a rudimentary stone shelter erected in an almost completely barren mountain basin at about six thousand five hundred feet, dominated on three sides by ridges behind which anyone with a rifle—"

"We shall get to all of that later," Canal cut him off. "None of that sort of thing before we break bread," he explained as he poured wine for both of them. "Tell me first about the letters."

Geoffrey, who had been convinced that the details of the rendezvous site were of the utmost importance and would play a determinant role in their ability to guarantee Hélissenne's and their own safety, balked at this change of topic. "Don't you think," he began, looking Canal right in the eye, "we should work out some of the details of the exchange right away?"

"You never know which details will be important and which will be irrelevant at the outset," pontificated the retired secret serviceman, as he sized his lunch mate up, looking for signs of ready intelligence in his face. "What seems most pressing at first may turn out to be utterly superfluous," he continued, doing his best to be persuasive. "Let us proceed by order. Your predicament has arisen from what you found, so tell me first about what you found—tell me about the letters."

Yielding to the older and supposedly wiser man's wishes, Geoffrey answered, "Which letters? The older ones or the newer ones?"

"What do you mean? There are older ones and newer ones?"

"Yes, there are two separate packets of letters."

"You mean you have found versions of both the early love letters from around 1116 and the later letters from around 1132?"

Geoffrey noted that the inspector seemed to be extremely well informed about the correspondence between Heloise and Abelard. "No," he replied, "we found what appears to be a complete version of the early love letters along with a faithful copy of them made at a significantly later date."

"How much later?"

"The apparent copyist wrote January 1543 on the last page of the copy, followed by the initials M-d-M and M.d.N."

"Interesting," Canal said, scratching his chin as he filed away the details for later contemplation. "And have you examined the paper for corroborating watermarks and fabrication details?"

"We haven't. Unfortunately, neither of us knows very much about parchments, paper manufacturing techniques, inks, and so on."

"I see."

"Nevertheless," Geoffrey added, as if by way of compensation, "it is a highly legible and seemingly faithful copy of the older version, which consists of very faded ink on ancient, brittle parchment. Even without carbon dating the parchment, Hélissenne's impression was that it closely resembles the twelfth- and thirteenth-century parchments she has seen in libraries."

"Excellent, excellent. I should very much like to see both sets of letters immediately after lunch."

"No problem." Geoffrey's appreciation for Canal's enthusiasm and the arrival of their appetizer conspired to make him forget about getting straight to the purported point. Tasting the excellent wine, he dug with gusto into the salad with delicate French green beans and red onion.

"What I do not understand," Canal began anew after chewing meditatively for a spell, "is why you do not simply photograph all the pages of one set of letters with a date and time stamp, or copy one set of them and have the copy notarized to establish the priority of your find and original ownership. Then you could hand the other set over in exchange for Hélissenne. Is it the simplicity of the solution that stopped it from occurring to you?" the Frenchman asked, even though he did not for a split second believe this was the reason.

The American seemed a little dazed at first, but then resumed his chewing. "I have to admit, it hadn't occurred to me that they might not know there were two sets of letters. I had been tempted to give them only every other page or to cut each page in half, to render them useless to them."

"Yet in attacking the materiality of the letters, you would be rendering them less valuable to yourselves as well," Canal remarked, recalling all the ruckus he had once kicked up when he had claimed that a letter remained what it was even when cut into small pieces, and that letters could be *en souffrance*, even if he had never imagined inflicting suffering on them the way Geoffrey had in mind.

"True. But as you said, such measures may not be at all necessary since Hélissenne may have told her kidnappers nothing or as little as possible, and we might be able to hand over just one set of the letters to them in exchange for her."

Canal nodded. "And the older version would obviously be worth a great deal more, even if it is more difficult to read. A manuscript like that might fetch a great deal of money at—"

"We're far more interested in the scholarly value of the manuscript than in any sort of monetary gain," Geoffrey hastened to explain. "In any case," he added, "it is not at all clear that we are the rightful owners of the letters—they presumably belong to whoever owns the site, which, if I'm not mistaken, is the regional government." Here he gave Canal a knowing look. "And it is probably Monsieur Picard, the director of the archeological dig, who has the clearest right to publish the letters."

"The plot thickens." Canal mused for a few moments and then inquired, "If your primary concern is, as you say, for the scholarly value of the letters, are you somehow concerned that the thieves will not publish the letters?"

"I worry that they will be sold to the highest bidder, whether a private collector or library, and squirreled away rather than reaching their proper destination—the reading public."

"What makes you think *that* is their proper destination?"

"What else could it be?"

"Maybe their destination is no other than where they happen to be read at any particular moment in time, nothing more than the impact they may have on their current readers." Reading the American's blank features as expressing incomprehension, the Frenchman resorted to allegory. "When a man goes to a far-off place to escape from his problems," he began, "his problems always catch up with him sooner or later. Try as he might to forget them, they do not forget him. We might say, in such a case, that *their* destination is wherever *he* happens to be."

"What does that have to do with the letters?" the graduate student asked, visibly baffled.

"Perhaps they bring their destination with them wherever they go," Canal proffered, raising his eyebrows significantly at Geoffrey. "Their destination is, as it was once written, not their literal addressee, or even whoever possesses them, but whoever is possessed by them."

"Possessed by them?" the Midwesterner gulped, despite having neither dessert nor wine in his throat.

XVII

The Frenchman was crestfallen to hear at the end of lunch that Geoffrey had been unable to reserve a room for him in the hotel in Gincla, as the place was full to the brim, and that he would thus have to lodge in the far more modest accommodations of the archeological interns in Lapradelle. He was heartened, however, by Geoffrey's brisk offer to switch rooms with him—for even as unsubtle an observer of human emotions as Geoffrey could not fail to notice Canal's disappointment at the news. The inspector nonetheless declined the offer, and soon became completely absorbed in examining the older packet of letters.

The two men had laid the documents out on the desk in Geoffrey's room, and Canal quickly pointed out that whereas the vast majority of the text was written in what appeared to be a male hand, there were a few pages interspersed with the others written in a different hand, which to Canal's trained eye appeared to be feminine.

"So what of it?" said Geoffrey, to whom the significance of this was unclear.

"Well, you can see that the other letters are all copied one after the other without any break on the page, and—"

"Copied? I thought these were originals."

"They both are and are not, which is often the case with what one initially believes to be original texts," Canal explained, winking inwardly, if such a thing be possible. "Parchment was prohibitively expensive at the time and most letters between people—when they did not involve legal agreements—were written on wax tablets which could be heated and erased for reuse. Teachers and their students almost always communicated with each other in this way, and that is what Abelard and Heloise were to each other at the outset. Lovers did the same, employing a trusted servant as go-between to convey the tablets, usually wrapped in an embroidered bag of some kind, back and forth between the lovers."

"So you couldn't keep a copy of the message you had just received, because you would have to erase it to write your own message in its place."

"Yes," Canal agreed partially, "assuming there was insufficient room on the tablets to include your answer."

"But even if there were, you still wouldn't have your own copy of the letter to look at later."

"*Précisément*. Which is why people often kept a running log on parchment of both the letters they received and the letters they sent. That way they could read them again and again at their leisure, and would know what their beloved was responding to when next they received a letter from him or her."

"Sounds like it was the carbon copy or e-mail archive of the time."

The Frenchman nodded. "I reread the excerpted love letters published back in 1974 before I fell asleep last night, and Abelard says very clearly that he often reads Heloise's letters to him over and over again, suggesting that he himself kept a copy of their correspondence. Most scholars naively suggest that only Heloise would have kept a copy of the letters, as if love only concerned women!" Canal raised his eyebrows at Geoffrey.

The American seemed to share Canal's indignation at this insinuation.

"*She* almost certainly kept a copy, for she sometimes says she rereads his letters every hour and even kisses them. But here," Canal continued, holding up a few of the letters before them, "we have virtual proof that Abelard too copied most if not all of their letters to each other, except for these few that are written in a feminine hand. They were no doubt sent by Heloise on parchment because Abelard was far away at the time and wax tablets would have been too cumbersome or impractical to transport."

"That would explain why the prior letter sometimes ends not at the bottom of the previous page of parchment, but in the middle, and that the next letter begins on a new sheet of parchment." Geoffrey found a letter in the newer packet corresponding to that particular page and reread it quickly. "Yes, it is definitely from a woman—she calls her beloved *carissimo*."

Canal nodded approvingly.

"Why would scholars assume that Abelard wouldn't have been interested in keeping a record of their correspondence?"

"I guess they judge based on their own experience," Canal provided as a ready reply, having evidently pondered the question before, "and finding themselves not—or at least no longer—terribly interested in love, assume that Abelard could not have been either, even though he wrote hundreds of love songs about Heloise that were sung in France for generations." He pushed his chair back, reflected for a moment, and then added, "You might say that it is the counterpart of that other stupidity invented in the twentieth century by twits like Georges Duby that no woman could possibly have written the letters allegedly by Heloise and that a man, whether it was Abelard or not, must have written *both sides* of the correspondence."

"Sounds like they can't decide whether only women are interested in love or only men," Geoffrey laughed. "A bit too much of an either/or perhaps."

Canal appreciated the irony too and laughed heartily at the absurdity of introducing the vel of exclusion in such a context.

The inspector rose to stretch and gazed out the window at the lovely mountain scenery. Geoffrey took advantage of the pause to disappear for a couple of minutes to get a bottle of sparkling water, which he was badly in need of, having drunk considerably more wine than he was used to.

Pouring the bubbly into glasses, he expressed a thought that had obviously occurred to him peripatetically in the interim, "I imagine Abelard would've kept a copy of their correspondence for other reasons too. He comes off in his autobiography as like a blogger who thinks everything he pens is so fabulous it should be published for all the world to see. Personally, I suspect he thought that these letters would one day become famous."

"If he did," Canal remarked, eyeing Geoffrey closely, "he was awfully prescient, for his letters are far better known than anything else he ever wrote, even if he had an early idea of the distinction between the signifier and the signified."

"Did he really?" Geoffrey asked, genuinely impressed. "I thought no one had had the slightest inkling of that before the twentieth century."

"Abelard differentiated *voces* from *sermones*," Canal replied, nodding. Then he added, "Your suspicion might help explain why he encouraged Heloise to turn their love letter writing into a kind of competition in which they would rival with each other to see who could write the most original greetings and who could express love for the other in the most extravagant terms. It always struck me as like one of those odd disputes certain couples get into about who loves who more, each one claiming to love more than the other loves in return."

"I've always found that rather nauseating myself. 'I love you more than anyone has ever loved anyone else.' 'No, I love you infinitely, schnookums,'" Geoffrey said, imitating first a female voice and then a male one.

"Yes, quite hard to believe. The more you proclaim extreme love from every mountaintop, the more likely it is that it is not really genuine and that you are simply trying to convince yourself and others that it is."

Geoffrey was somewhat shaken by this declaration by the Frenchman, who seemed to him to speak with considerable authority. "Do you really think that is true? Then you're not so sure Heloise and Abelard really loved each other?"

"I did not say that. But I do think we see signs, especially in their early letters, that they were also in love with being in love. More strongly, perhaps at times, than they were in love with each other." The inspector scrutinized the graduate student and noticed his discomfort. "Did something I said upset you?"

"No," Geoffrey said evasively. "I just …," he uttered and then broke off for some moments. "Hélissenne is constantly telling me how much she loves me, so maybe she's mostly in love with being in love. But somehow I don't think so. And I think she wishes I would proclaim my love more often than I do."

"You do it less often than she does?"

"Not the first few weeks. I fell head over heels in love with her right away and constantly told her how much I loved her. But the last week or so, I don't know … I guess I've been feeling sort of annoyed with her or something."

Canal sat in silence, waiting for him to go on.

"Or maybe I've been annoyed with myself for spending all my time with her and thinking about her and reading up on her interests."

"Meanwhile neglecting your own research?"

"How did you know?" the American asked, surprised for the third time by the Frenchman's suppositions.

"Finding the letters changed that because they suddenly seemed to make up for having gotten nowhere with *your* research? Being with Hélissenne and making a name for yourself magically stopped being incompatible projects for a few days?"

"If that," Geoffrey ejaculated. Feeling that he had said more than he should have, he suddenly regarded Canal sheepishly. "It's embarrassing to say, really."

Canal nodded, listening intently.

The young man finally spoke again, "I wouldn't say that I was *relieved* when Hélissenne went missing, but—"

"But you just did," the inspector commented, wondering to himself how anyone could be taken in by retractions, especially those by people named Geoffrey.

XVIII

On the morrow, the Frenchman and the American spent the morning in Canal's room on the top floor of the hotel in Lapradelle poring over every detail of the kidnapping as well as photographing and copying both sets of letters. They cut off small pieces of the parchment and paper used in the different packets and sent them to a laboratory in Paris that Canal knew for carbon dating. Having detected watermarks on the newer packet of letters, they carefully measured, sketched, and photographed them. A quick visit to a notary allowed them to secure written proof that they had a certified copy and to attest to the date and time of their "possession" of the documents, whether such possession happened to be legal or not. They resolved to bring both packets with them to the Cabane de la Balmette, but to offer Hélissenne's abductors solely the newer packet in exchange for Hélissenne at first and then follow their lead.

But what to make of the threat note? The paper offered no clues and the font and even the generic writing itself indicated little other than that the author was a native English speaker. There were plenty of such speakers in Hélissenne's entourage, though Geoffrey barely knew any of them since they were not really friends of hers, and there were of course dozens of English-speaking tourists who visited Puilaurens Castle every day.

It was not clear whether the author had adopted the royal or the collective "we" in his threatening missive. But the fact that Geoffrey's room had been ransacked, even though Madame Cochenille was sure the alleged friend from America could not have gone upstairs to the rooms, led them to conclude that they would probably be facing at least two assailants during the exchange in the mountains. The hotelier had confirmed that several new people had checked into the hotel the day Geoffrey's room had been broken into, but none of them were native English speakers as far as she could tell, and Geoffrey had not had a chance to get a glimpse of any of them thus far since they were out and about whenever he was around.

Canal remarked that since, according to the hotelier, the English-speaker's French was quite good, he might even have been able to enlist the services of a member of the hotel staff, which did little to help them narrow the field of potential assailants they might encounter.

Discussing all of this in Canal's room, Geoffrey noticed that the inspector constantly spoke as if he too would be coming to the Cabane de la Balmette.

"The note clearly states that I have to go to the meeting place alone," Geoffrey reminded him, even though he would have been more than happy to have backup.

"Yes, meaning zat it has to appear to the kidnappers that you have come alone."

"Just appear?"

"Yes, that should suffice."

"You have a notion about the way in which those appearances could be deceiving?"

"I do, as a matter of fact," Canal said, winking.

Geoffrey waited for the retired inspector to go on.

"I can think of at least two different scenarios, neither of which requires us to involve the police, who do not seem terribly interested in the first place and might complicate matters regarding title to the letters in the second."

"Do you think your scenarios would guarantee we actually get Hélissenne back in exchange for the letters?"

"Is that what you want?" Canal inquired, only partially tongue-in-cheek.

"It is," Geoffrey said with resolve. "I know I said that her absence was sort of a relief yesterday, but I realize now how much she means to me. It helped to realize that I was taking out my own annoyance at myself on her."

Canal nodded. "Yes, sometimes it is enough to simply hear oneself say these things to somebody else to get past them," he said aloud, adding "at least for a while" to himself.

"So what are these two scenarios of yours?"

"Well, one depends on the availability of sheep. Did you notice any sheep, sheep droppings, or bells ringing when you went up to check out the meeting place?"

Geoffrey was stumped. "I didn't pay any attention ...," he began. "I was so caught up in castigating myself for abusing Hélissenne's trust by convincing her to return to the castle that night, something she never would have considered doing. It's all my fault! I pushed, I wheedled, I caused her downfall," he continued, oblivious to parataxis, "something perhaps irremediable."

"The girl's not dead, you knucklehead," Canal quipped affectionately yet firmly, placing his hand on the young man's forearm. "We will find her, and everything will be all right."

Geoffrey bowed his head and the inspector renewed his request, "Now what about sheep?" He sat in silence, giving the student time to cast his mind back to his hike the day before last.

Geoffrey eventually did speak. "I can't say as I noticed any sheep droppings, but then I don't have a terribly good idea of what they look like—I mostly know cow pies and horse apples."

Canal nodded, thinking to himself, "Typical city boy." No one had yet told him that Geoffrey had grown up in a small town in the Midwest.

"But I did notice a faint tinkling of bells off in the distance, kind of like the wind chimes people hang out on their porches back home."

Canal was pleased. "So there are flocks of sheep up there, and it would not be so unusual for a shepherd to be walking about."

"I guess not, though it might be unusual for a shepherd to be walking around up there without any sheep."

"There is that. I would have to borrow some, which could be a bit difficult on such short notice. Still, I suspect that with the proper inducements and gratifications ..."

"Which are precisely what I can't offer many of," Geoffrey hastened to mention.

"*Qu'à cela ne tienne!*" Seeing no comprehension on the American's face, the Frenchman translated loosely, "There is no need to worry about that."

"Oh, but I do."

"That leads us to system B—no, I think you Americans call it plan B."

"What is plan B?"

"Plan B involves a certain elderly gentleman with a long flowing beard, beret, meerschaum pipe, and overstuffed backpack hiking into the area around the Cabane at least an hour before you are expected there."

Geoffrey's face registered perplexity.

The inspector pointed to his old-fashioned rucksack in the corner of the room and then extracted a fake beard from a nearby suitcase.

As the picture of plan B began to come into focus for Geoffrey, objections to it began to form in his mind. "I don't mean to offend," he began, "but—"

"And yet the idea of offending came to mind," Canal stated steadfastly. "Perhaps you do mean to offend?"

"All I'm saying," Geoffrey waved off this tangent, which to him was tantamount to niggling, "is that you might not prove much of a match for two or more men my age, especially if they have rifles."

"I would not bet on it if I were you. I can still hit a crow at a hundred paces," Canal said, removing a shiny pistol from his inside jacket holster. "Standard issue in the French secret services, although I did have it modified a few years back to ... well, let us just say to improve its overall performance."

Geoffrey was impressed, excited, and scared at the implications of their plan all at the same time. "Do you mind if I have a look at it?" he asked timorously.

"Go right ahead," Canal said, standing up. "It is not loaded. Will you excuse me for a moment?" he asked, gesturing toward the door. "I need to use the facilities."

"Of course," Geoffrey said, looking up from the gun in his hands.

XIX

"Does your Hélissenne have any birthmarks or moles that you can recall?" Canal asked as he re-entered the room where Geoffrey was still sitting, cradling the gun.

This query startled the graduate student, who had had multiple scenarios of violent Alpine confrontations running through his head during the inspector's absence.

"Have you noticed any freckles or scars on her legs or arms?" Canal persisted.

Geoffrey appeared to make a serious effort at picturing Hélissenne in his mind, closing his eyes to focus better. With his eyes still shut, he eventually proffered, "If I'm not mistaken, she has a cute little mole, like a tiny chocolate chip, on the second toe of her left foot."

"I need you to come have a look at something," Canal said, opening the door a few inches and positioning Geoffrey so that he could look through the crack. "A girl is going to walk by in a minute or two, and I want you to look at her feet very closely."

Geoffrey was still more confused now than before. "What for?"

"There is something not quite right about a girl whom I have passed in the hall several times now on the way to the bathroom. Every time I greet her, she responds in the same automatic, faraway voice, and when I asked her just now what brought her here, she said she was a tourist."

"What's so unusual about that? This is a well-known tourist region, after all, isn't it?"

"What is so unusual about it is that she never seems to leave her room except to use the shower or restroom down the hall. And she never goes to the dining room."

"Maybe she's tired of visiting and brought some food up to her room."

"Maybe. But she left her door ajar on the way to the shower a minute ago and I peeked into her room," Canal admitted unabashedly. "She has no luggage, no clothes, no camera, no passport, no money, nothing."

"Hmm."

"She does not look anything like the pictures of Hélissenne you showed me. This girl has red hair and wears ultramodern tinted glasses. But she is about Hélissenne's height and—"

"A lot of girls are about Hélissenne's height."

"And speaks French with no accent."

"So? Plenty of French girls speak their native tongue with no noticeable accent, from what I've heard."

"So both last night and early this morning, a man with an American accent knocked at her door and called Melissa, as if that were her name. Now Melissa is hardly a French name, even if in recent years some people have started giving their kids all kinds of American names."

"And she answered to that name?"

"Not when *I* said it a minute ago. Twice she opened the door to the man I overheard when *he* said it—it stuck in my mind because he woke me up with his loud voice at an ungodly hour this morning," the inspector complained. "But when I said

'*Bonjour Melissa*' just now, she walked by as if she had not even heard what I—"

"She *has* a mole on the second toe of her left foot," Geoffrey whispered excitedly, having just seen the girl walk by Canal's door in a bathrobe and thongs.

XX

"Did they look like Hélissenne's feet?" the inspector inquired.

"Yes, but of course I can't be absolutely sure they are."

"Of course?"

"Well I have to admit I have never studied her feet all that closely."

"You tend to focus more on other parts of her body?" Canal asked, smiling at the corners of his mouth.

Geoffrey ignored the sexual insinuation and replied, "I'm sure I know her face and hands much better than her feet."

"Her face and hands and nothing else?"

"I have, naturally, noticed her general shape through her clothing."

"I see," Canal remarked, stroking his chin, struck by the relatively unusual absence of carnal relations between two people from their backgrounds and age group who were ostensibly in love, especially between two people who actually saw each other regularly in the flesh, unlike the hordes of "internaughties" who so often confined themselves to virtual relations. "And what about the shape of the girl you just saw?"

"You mentioned her feet, so I mostly looked at her feet," Geoffrey protested, feeling slightly chastened.

"Mostly?"

"Well, I did get a glimpse of her torso too, but in a plush bathrobe like that it's pretty hard to divine anything."

"Then we will have to obtain further confirmation. We will need to stake out her room," the Frenchman opined, thinking out loud. "I shall wait down the hall and you keep an eye out from here."

"Why not just knock at her door? If it's Hélissenne, she'll recognize my voice and let us in."

"I doubt it, but you can give it a try anyway. I will keep a lookout at the top of the stairs to make sure no one comes along and sees you."

Exiting the room, the inspector went to the stairs, listened for a moment, and gave Geoffrey the thumbs up. Geoffrey confined himself first to simply knocking, and then called Hélissenne's name several times to no avail. He eventually tried calling Melissa a couple of times to no better effect, and finally began entreating Hélissenne to open the door in Latin.

Not only was he thoroughly unsuccessful, but there was no sound of any kind whatsoever from behind the door. Dismayed, Geoffrey approached the inspector. "Now what?" he asked.

Canal had been thinking about how to approach the girl while he was standing guard and observing Geoffrey's futile enterprise. "I will stay over here," he whispered, "and you watch from inside my room with the door ajar a few inches. When she comes out again to go to the bathroom, you come out of my room and accost her—that way you can get a good look at her face. I will come up from behind and jostle her, accidentally on purpose, and try to see if that red hair of hers is a wig or not."

"Sounds like a plan. But I still don't quite get it. Her kidnappers might have simply moved her two floors up from her original room?"

"You have to admit that you yourself never thought of looking for her in the very same room two floors up."

"And they might have disguised her like that?"

"Who would have thought of looking for a redhead with yellow-tinted glasses? Certainly not the police, if you had given them the same description you gave me and shown them the same pictures you showed me."

"No, I guess not."

"You have read Edgar Allan Poe's *Purloined Letter*, have you not?" inquired the inspector. Geoffrey nodded. "It is ze same basic principle employed by the minister to hide the letter he pilfered from the Queen's boudoir."

"I think I see what you mean," Geoffrey said after a few moments of reflection. "The minister hid the letter in plain sight, disguising it in such a way that it couldn't possibly fit the description of it given to the police who were commissioned to find it."

"Are any of the English-speaking interns fans of American literature or psychoanalysis?"

"Psychoanalysis?" Geoffrey queried, mystified by this reference to such a seemingly extraneous field.

"I believe that a few prominent analysts have discussed the story over the years."

"As far as I know, all the native English speakers among the interns are medievalists."

"Hmm," Canal grunted. "The twist here compared to Poe's story seems to be that we are not dealing with an inanimate object." He paused for a moment and then added, "Maybe seeing you right in front of her nose will have some effect on her."

Geoffrey was unable to follow the other's train of thought. "How do you mean?"

"She speaks in a funny way, as though she were in some sort of somnambulistic trance," Canal began. "And she appeared not to recognize your voice. In a word, she has been disguised on the inside as well as on the outside."

XXI

As the interminable minutes and then hours rolled by, the never-ending stakeout began to seem futile. Geoffrey felt less and less convinced that Canal's mysterious neighbor was in fact Hélissenne, whether camouflaged on the outside, the inside, or both. A man had come to the door to deliver a tray of food to the alleged Melissa around one, reminding Geoffrey that he hadn't had a bite to eat for many an hour and soon wouldn't be able to find any real sustenance anywhere, all the local restaurants ceasing to seat diners after two in the afternoon.

Canal, who had quickly hidden in a linen closet on a few occasions when people had ventured as high up as the top floor, appeared unflappably impassive, giving Geoffrey an even greater sense that time was a-wasting. Hélissenne had been missing for three days at this point, and he could contact the police and try to get things moving. For all the good publicity he had heard about this inspector, perhaps he was, Geoffrey fumed, just another one of those lazy, good-for-nothing French functionaries who did as little as possible between two-hour lunches and three-hour dinners.

Lost in such ungrateful thought, Geoffrey almost missed his chance of accosting the girl—who, he felt, had no doubt had time to lunch leisurely, read a magazine lackadaisically from cover to cover, and nap comfortably by now—when she finally began her short journey down the hall to use the restroom. Deviating from the agreed upon plan, the American rushed out into the hall and inadvertently collided with her with so much force that what turned out to be a wig flew off. As she hurriedly bent over to pick it up, her ill-fitting yellow-tinted glasses fell to the ground. Geoffrey, who banged his head against hers as he bent down to help her retrieve them, found himself, even as he rubbed his head, gazing into those hazel eyes he knew so well, even if the official name of their color was still somewhat unfamiliar to him.

The dewigging had revealed long, flowing chestnut-colored hair, and the expression on Geoffrey's face was enough to convince the inspector that the American was no longer unsure as to the identity of the mystery guest lodged in the room across the hall from Canal's.

Geoffrey enthusiastically repeated her name, but seemed to become paralyzed when she failed to return his gaze, and especially when she hurried off down the hall after gathering her things from the floor. Canal sprang into action and quickly pushed both of them into his room and locked the door behind them. The lithesome girl resisted for a few moments and then, losing the poise that usually lent her an air of quiet elegance, went somewhat limp on the chair. Her eyes, which in her current state had lost all of their usual refulgence, were half-closed and her breathing became labored.

The American too was in a sorry state, seeming to take it personally that she had failed to acknowledge him or call his name. "How come she doesn't know me?" he whined. "How could she fail to recognize me? If she really loved me, she'd—"

Canal put a stop to this runaway train of disconsolate thoughts. "She has obviously been hypnotized, you big baby. She has been instructed not to recognize anyone other than her

104

abductors and to say no more than a few perfunctory words to anyone else."

"But if I really meant something to her, none of that would make any difference," insisted Geoffrey. "Would it?" he added after a few seconds, seeing the inspector's resolute face.

"Hypnosis is very serious business. We are going to have to find a way to get her to snap out of it. So stop playing the wounded suitor and start thinking."

XXII

The striking French girl had lost all tonus. She slumped backward in the spartan wood chair furnished by the hotel in what appeared to be a very uncomfortable position. Canal corralled Geoffrey's and his own efforts to move her on the chair toward the wall so as to prop her up and help her breathe more easily, her head now falling neither backward nor forward.

Examining her soft features closely, the inspector first tried snapping his fingers and clapping his hands loudly in front of her to try to awaken her from her trance. This availing little, if at all—her eyelids barely fluttered momentarily after each noise—he turned to his companion to see if he had any ideas.

Geoffrey began speaking loudly to Hélissenne, first in Latin, then in English, and finally in something that sounded to Canal's ears rather like French, which astonished the inspector as he had gotten the distinct impression that the American did not speak any French at all. When Canal asked him about this, Geoffrey admitted that he had been spending a couple of hours every morning studying French and practicing with various members of the hotel staff, hoping to surprise Hélissenne with his newly acquired ability to understand and speak a little of her mother tongue. He fretted aloud that Hélissenne was refusing to respond because she was angry at him, they having parted last on somewhat ambiguous terms, but Canal assured him that this was not likely to be the problem.

The inspector next tried to dehypnotize or rehypnotize Hélissenne, first speaking directly into her ear in a low, forceful voice designed to entrance and, when that failed, dangling a pocket watch in front of her eyes while Geoffrey tried to hold her eyelids open. The hope was to put her into yet another altered state by which to combat the first, but the first foiled all of their efforts.

"Whoever is after those letters," Canal remarked, "went all out, for they seem to have employed a specialist."

"What can we do?"

"You could always try the ardent kissing approach," Canal replied offhandedly.

Geoffrey required no coaxing—he immediately pressed his lips to the girl's, pale though they were in her abstracted state, and gave it the old college try.

Breathing hard, he backed away and looked at her cherished face closely. He seemed still further dejected after noticing no difference whatsoever and sunk down onto the bed.

Canal paced back and forth near the window, deep in thought.

Geoffrey finally broke the silence, proposing that they force the girl to drink until she was so drunk the spell would dissipate. The Frenchmen did not reject the proposition out of hand, but observed that in her current state, it might be difficult to get her to actually swallow anything they put in her mouth.

"What I think we should try first," the inspector eventually declared, "is to guess the word that will break the spell. Hypnotists very often provide their subjects with a specific word or phrase, which when uttered will awaken them from the somnambulistic state."

"Sounds like a potentially infinite task. Wouldn't we have to pronounce aloud every word and expression in the dictionary?"

"Certainly not *every* word. Only words or expressions that are rarely used, so that the person would not be awakened accidentally, but only when the hypnotist so desired."

"Words in Latin too, you think?"

"I highly doubt any professional hypnotist speaks a dead language like Latin well enough to induce a hypnotic trance or provide specific instructions. And you told me that Hélissenne's English is nothing to write home about, so I think we can safely assume that the operation must have been conducted in French."

Canal continued his musings aloud, "It could be a somewhat technical term like *désenvoûtement*, but that might easily come up in the context of a discussion of how to awaken her. It could be an abstruse term from almost any field, whether *chevillé* from carpentry, *automatisme de répétition* from psychoanalysis, *flux de chaleur* from thermodynamics, or what have you."

None of these sample technical terms had even the slightest effect on Hélissenne, not that the inspector had expected them to, leading Canal to go on with his audible ruminations. "It could also be some rare phrase from literature, like *substantifique moëlle*, or from baby talk, like *caca boudin* ..."

"Or something from children's comic books," Geoffrey joined in the soliloquy, "like *mille millions de mille sabords* or *saperlipopette*."

At this latter sound, Canal noticed that Hélissenne's eyelids genuinely flickered for the first time. Geoffrey's pronunciation of Tintin's favorite, but seriously outdated, interjection had not been terribly exact, so the inspector quickly repeated it more loudly and with a typical French, rather than either American or Belgian, accent.

Lo and behold, Hélissenne's eyes opened!

Tonic posture returning to her frame, she sat up straight and looked at the inspector, bewildered. Geoffrey was not in her immediate field of vision, and she exclaimed in French, "Who are you? Where am I?"

"*C'est un ami à moi,*" Geoffrey explained in the best French accent he could muster, jumping up from the bed and hugging the newly reanimated girl excitedly.

Hélissenne pushed him away, not having recognized Geoffrey's voice as it spoke French, and then, catching a glimpse of his face, she pulled him back toward her and clasped him eagerly in her supple arms.

"*Geoffroi, mon amour,*" she exclaimed, and tears flowed down her cheeks. "Where have you been?" she continued in French, caught up in the emotion. "What is going on?!"

"Someone hypnotized you," Geoffrey replied. "You have actually been here in the hotel all along, but in a room on a different floor." His pronunciation and grammar were sketchy, but comprehensible enough, given the circumstances.

Canal, who had been waiting for the touching scene of reunion to conclude, now introduced himself to Hélissenne as a retired secret services inspector whom Geoffrey had hired to help find Hélissenne who had been missing since Monday.

"Monday?" asked Hélissenne nervously. "What day is it?"

"It's Thursday," Geoffrey replied.

"Thursday?" she exclaimed, panicking. "It isn't Sunday?" She paused for a moment to take inventory of her recollections. "I don't remember anything beyond Sunday night. After you dropped me off at the hotel, I went into my room, turned on the light, and found three men in there waiting to ambush me. One of them locked the door and the other two tied me to a chair and gagged me."

"I'll kill them!" cried Geoffrey who certainly didn't understand every word, but managed to get the gist.

"Did you recognize any of them?" the inspector asked calmly.

"It was Randolph, that obnoxious graduate student from Harvard," she said with a disgusted look on her face, "and a couple of guys he had obviously paid to do his bidding."

"Can you describe them to us?"

"There was a coarse looking French guy built like a bouncer—"

"That must be the one who brought up lunch today," Canal reflected out loud.

"And an older Frenchman with very strange eyes," she said, shivering, "and an even stranger way of speaking."

"He must have been the hypnotist they brought in."

"They demanded I hand over the letters, but I said I didn't have them. The last thing I remember," she went on, "was suddenly feeling very drowsy, like I couldn't keep my eyes open."

XXIII

The evening and the morning and the next day. Canal surveyed the work that had been done thus far and saw that it was good but by no means finished. The girl had been retrieved and brought back to herself, but their adversaries, while down, were probably not out. They would soon discover Hélissenne's absence and would likely, given the determination they had thus far shown, come up with a new plan of attack. This one might be more violent and more decisive.

Finding Randolph and making a preemptive strike seemed, however, to be the furthest thing from the two lovers' minds. Having concluded that Hélissenne could not safely stay at her hotel in Lapradelle, for the nonce at least, she agreed to go with Geoffrey to his hotel in Gincla. It was not clear to Canal whether they intended to find a separate room for her or to spend the night in the same room, but in any case he noted that they did not bother to call the hotel first to see if any accommodations had become available for Hélissenne, much less for the inspector himself.

Canal's discreet inquiries about Randolph's whereabouts to the hotel staff at the front desk and other archeological interns who lived on the same floor as him suggested that he had been in and out as usual over the past few days—no doubt, Canal mused, all the better to deflect suspicion from himself. The inspector kept an eye out for Randolph throughout dinner, but no one even remotely fitting his description joined the other interns at their tables at the far end of the restaurant. Rather than camp out on his doorstep on the third floor of the hotel, thereby arousing the curiosity of Randolph's friends—if he had any—or potential accomplices, Canal resolved to confront him directly at the archeological dig the following morning.

XXIV

When Hélissenne awoke, the sun was shining, the birds were singing, and she felt marvelous, having spent a passionate, sensuous, and tender evening and night with her beloved. The experience had differed vastly from the first nights she had spent with the other two boys she had known, for she was truly in love with Geoffrey and felt that he was no less truly in love with her.

It was the first time she felt no shame whatsoever at having slept with a boy—she wanted to be his all, his everything, his one and only, body, mind, heart, and soul. She had held nothing back and had not felt for a moment like she should. It had seemed to Hélissenne that to her prior lovers—no, she could not call them that, for they had been mere flirtations—it was a game to see who would give what, how much, and how soon, to see who would conquer and who would fall.

None of that had been at stake this time. There had been no games, no waiting to see what move the other would make. He had taken her and she had given herself to him unconditionally.

She turned away from the window to look at her beloved beside her and great was her surprise to find the bed empty. Where could he have gone? Probably just to the bathroom, she told herself, and then listened intently for any sound that might be coming out of the private bathroom. But no sound was to be heard.

"Geoffroi, my total love," she called, but there was no answer. He's probably just gone down to get the paper, she reflected, but was unhappy with the thought that he might want to read the paper on such a morning as this.

As the minutes dragged by, the merry tweeting of the birds began to grate on her, and the rays of sunshine streaming in through the window began to feel like a reproachful finger pointing at her. Had she merely been deluding herself? Perhaps Geoffrey had not, in fact, been feeling what she herself had been feeling.

But his touch said otherwise. Words, she knew, could hide a good deal, and she had met men who could sweet-talk the pants off many a lass but were as unreliable as weather reports. Geoffrey's honeyed words had been ambrosia to her, but his sighs and looks and caresses had touched her even more deeply. They had seemed sure and true, and never for a moment during the torrid night had it crossed her mind to doubt them.

And still Geoffrey did not return. Had she lured herself into believing he truly loved her when he had simply been drunk with desire for her body, enamored of her feminine allurements? Ever so reluctantly, Hélissenne rose from what had to her resembled *l'Île des plaisirs*, dressed, and went down to the dining room where she suspected her beloved must be.

He wasn't. Madame Cochenille at the front desk had seen him go out toward his car about a half-hour before, but had not seen him since. Hélissenne hid from her the despair that seized her upon hearing this news, but gave full rein to it the moment she turned to go back upstairs to Geoffrey's room—to what had so fleetingly been *their* room.

Perhaps he had wanted to make himself the very center of her existence, her very life and breath, only so as to possess her and then dump her. Maybe what she had taken to be

116

the poetic outpouring of his desire to wrench her away from everyone and everything was but a strategy of conquest. The phrase "divide and conquer" flitted through her mind, and she smiled at the bitter irony that military metaphors were so often applied to affairs of the heart.

The hotel room was not small, but she began to feel the walls were too close. She couldn't breathe! She flung wide the windows and drank in the cool morning air of the mountains. Her eyes were drawn to the soft, green, tree-covered peaks nearby, and from there to the valleys leading down into the village. The sun reflected blindingly off the windshields of the cars in the parking lot before her, and she suddenly distinguished Geoffrey's car among them. There was something uncanny about its presence there, for she had assumed that Geoffrey must have driven off somewhere. And, stranger still, the trunk was open.

Wherever he had gone off to, he obviously had not gone by car, but why then had he opened the trunk? Perhaps he had left on foot to think about things and had taken something out of the car first. Being in what she presumed to be a distrait state of mind, he had no doubt simply forgotten to close the trunk. Still, she reflected, that was rather unlike him. He was, after all, *un peu maniaque* and generally had all his wits about him—indeed, at times, too many wits for her taste.

Curious despite her chagrin, she left the room, descended the stairs anew, exited the hotel, and crossed over to the parking lot slowly, meditatively, devoid of conviction.

She was flabbergasted by what she found. The car keys were dangling from the trunk lock and in the trunk itself was a note that read as follows:

Nous savons ce que vous avez. Nous avons ce que vous savez.
Si vous y tenez, venez l'échanger contre la chose à midi demain à la Cabane de la Balmette.
Venez seule, sinon ne comptez plus jamais le revoir vivant.

It wasn't clear whether relief or fright took hold more thoroughly of Hélissenne. Her Geoffrey had not left her, jilted her, abandoned her—rather, he had been kidnapped, most likely by the very same people who had hypnotized her. Why he had gone out to the car and opened the trunk—if, indeed, he was the one who had done so—she did not know, and it bothered her that he had even left the bed in which they had held each other, much less the room whose four walls had contained so many of her joys. She consoled herself with the thought that he, no doubt, had simply wanted to retrieve something from the car and fully intended to return to her in a matter of seconds.

Somewhat dazed, she leaned against the car for support and her eyes fell anew upon the paper she was still holding in her hand. She would have to hand over the letters at the exact same remote mountain location Geoffrey had been instructed to go to in the note he had received while she was in her trance. Otherwise she would risk never seeing him alive again!

XXV

It had been agreed that Canal would go to the Puilaurens Castle with Hélissenne on Friday morning so that she could show him both where she had found the letters and who Randolph was, if he had not already figured it out at dinner Thursday night. The inspector had, consequently, not yet left his hotel in Lapradelle, despite the tardive hour, at the point at which the Poitevine telephoned from Gincla.

When, in an anxious tone of voice, she read Canal the note she had found in Geoffrey's car, having been astonished by his prolonged absence from the room, the inspector was sorry that he had not been able to confront Randolph directly. The only boon was that his face would still be unknown to the unscrupulous graduate student and his previous plan of pretending to be a shepherd or a greybeard hiker might still be practicable. And given the short amount of time before the exchange was to occur, they would not have much time to come up with anything else short of kidnapping Randolph themselves.

Hélissenne admitted that she could not be sure what she had told Randolph and his partners in crime, since she had been under hypnosis, and realized that they might therefore have to give up both sets of letters. But unlike Geoffrey, she manifested no reluctance whatsoever to hand the two packets over to their adversaries, obviously weighing her beloved far more heavily in the balance than the prestige of publishing important historical documents for the first time. Randolph had perhaps reasoned—and rightly so, Canal reflected—that the girl would be more likely to instantaneously comply with his demands than the boy was.

It seemed to the inspector that there was a very good chance Randolph would forgo hypnosis and disguise this time and employ something closer to brute force, dragging Geoffrey up into the mountains and physically detaining him there overnight until the designated rendezvous time. Hélissenne and Canal would thus have little chance of stumbling upon Geoffrey hidden away somewhere nearby, merely dressed up as someone he was not. A potentially violent confrontation at six thousand feet looked unavoidable.

Since Hélissenne did not express the same misgivings about Randolph's intentions as her beloved had, seeming to assume Randolph would surrender Geoffrey to her unharmed in exchange for the letters, Canal conveyed none of his suspicions to her. To her it all seemed quite straightforward and Canal figured there was no need to alarm her in advance— there would be plenty of time for alarm later. He expressed to her his regret that they had not simply left town, as he had suggested might be wise the previous afternoon, but she seemed to have no regrets about having spent the night where and how she had spent it.

They agreed that Canal would join her at Geoffrey's hotel where they would develop a plan of action, one that would likely resemble, in most respects, the one the Frenchman had previously worked out with the American, little having changed apart from the kidnapped party.

XXVI

"Take a look at this," Hélissenne said excitedly. The inspector had arrived at the hotel in Gincla and had found her deeply engrossed in reading the letters she and Geoffrey had uncovered, piles of pages strewn all over the large table in the dining room she had commandeered. Canal had initially walked over and stood by silently for some moments, watching her read, until she looked up and greeted him cordially, inviting him to take a seat next to her at the table.

She pointed to a passage in both the twelfth-century original and the sixteenth-century copy. "Abelard is clearly beside himself here—Heloise has just told him to stop writing to her because she cannot bear for him to reproach her anymore." (The two native-born French speakers conversed in French, not Latin, but we shall follow their discussion in plain English.)

"Yes," the inspector nodded, "it is a crucial part of the correspondence. It seems that Abelard is taking out on Heloise his frustration with himself for having become obsessed with her," Canal continued, happy to have the opportunity to voice some of his own speculations about the correspondence. "He cannot accept the fact that he has given himself over completely to his sexual desire for her and has ended up seriously neglecting his philosophical work. It has led him to get angry at her for

121

every little thing, as if he were looking for a reason to break up with her."

Hélissenne brushed her exceedingly long hair back from her forehead and eyed the inspector closely. "So you noticed that too?"

Canal nodded and proffered, "Men do that sort of thing often enough."

"I wouldn't know," Hélissenne commented evasively. She pointed again at the passage in the original letter. "You see how different the handwriting is here from that found in the earlier and later letters." Canal indicated that he did. "It seems like he's so worked up, his hand is trembling as he claims she must not have loved him very much if she could throw his love away so easily and accuses her of just looking for some reason to sever their relations."

"A classic case of projection, if ever I saw one."

"Hmm," Hélissenne murmured, scrutinizing the inspector's face. "It seems to provide pretty conclusive proof that this copy of the letters was made by Abelard, not by Heloise."

"Quite right. We also noted," Canal included Geoffrey in the discovery, "a few letters here and there in a feminine hand. They appear to be letters that Heloise sent to Abelard directly on parchment, not on wax tablets."

"I don't know if you noticed," Hélissenne added with increasing zest, pleased to discourse with such a knowledge-able interlocutor, "but those pages are also of a slightly differ-ent size than the others." She flipped to one such page that she had turned sideways in the pile, and held it up for him to see in the light against the page after it, which was written in a different hand.

Canal was impressed and admitted that they had not observed that. He extracted from his bag a heavily hand-annotated Latin and English version of the excerpted love letters, opened it to a bookmarked page, and showed Hélissenne that the parchment she had just shown him corresponded to letter sixty-nine in the published edition. Then he opened his volume to another bookmark and began flipping through the pages in the old version in front of them looking for something. "Since you are good at interpreting handwriting—"

"I never said that," she protested modestly, interrupting him.

"Well, you seem to be able to detect fluctuations in handwriting that might correspond to different emotions."

"Maybe here and there."

"I certainly was not trying to imply that you are a graphologist," the inspector hastened to add, observing his interlocutor keenly.

"Graphology has always struck me as a bunch of …," she trailed off, not seeming to find a suitable word for it.

"*Balivernes?*" Canal queried, offering her the French equivalent of *hogwash*. She nodded enthusiastically. "I have never understood," continued the inspector, "why the French think they can know virtually everything about people by examining their handwriting." They both laughed at the absurdity of it. "Well, I suppose," he remarked, "it is no worse than the Americans with their ever expanding battery of personality tests, scales, and questionnaires. Anyway, I meant you seem to be good at paleography."

He found the spot in the correspondence he was looking for. "Heloise complains here that Abelard has been neglecting her and my suspicion is that, although he is taken with Heloise, he has found a barmaid or chambermaid with whom to satisfy his more animal desires and has begun—"

Seeing the indignant look on Hélissenne's face, Canal interrupted himself to say, "Did I say something that shocked you?"

"No," she replied a bit disingenuously, "it's just a little hard to believe that one of the most famous lovers of all time was cheating on his beloved while wooing her in his letters."

"Cheating?" Canal repeated, trying the word on for size. "It is hard to know exactly what to call it in this case." Assembling his thoughts, he continued, "Abelard probably assumed at the outset that Heloise was off-limits, sexually speaking. He knew that, as a well-known teacher in the Church at the time, it would be frowned upon for him to marry. And I am sure he believed at first that a woman in Heloise's position would never agree to sexual relations outside of marriage. On top of that, her uncle was there to ensure—at least initially—that no funny business transpired between tutor and student."

"So you're saying that he didn't see any incompatibility between courting Heloise, making her fall in love with him, and sleeping with chambermaids?"

"Who says it was not Heloise who made him fall in love with her?" the inspector asked, winking at Hélissenne. "Love for him was, I think, partly a literary exercise, partly a captivating pastime, and partly a haven in a heartless world largely of his own making. To him, sex was a concession to the weakness of the flesh that he tried not to take seriously by indulging in it only occasionally with women beneath his rank whom he would never consider marrying. He obviously did not want to be captivated by a woman and, considering himself to be God's gift to all women, could not imagine depriving so many of his splendiferous self. Later he admits to Heloise that she managed to conquer him as no other woman had."

"You think he saw Heloise as his Lady, then, as if it were some sort of courtly love relationship?" asked the Poitevine, referring to the form of love practiced in certain courts in southwestern France starting not long before Abelard and Heloise's time.

"Not really. For that she would have had to have been married to someone else, which she was not, and of more exalted rank than him, which seems not to have been the case. Rather, I think she took their relationship far more seriously than he did, for while she often speaks of the bonds, chains,

124

and obligations of love, he never does. Even though he claims to have fallen in love with her before he even met her, just by hearing people talk about how cultured and refined she was, he seems to take their flirtation as something of a game, a delightful sublimation, a marvelous distraction from his tense rivalries and competitions with other philosophical and theological orators of the time, and from the political machinations in which he was enmeshed—or at least imagined he was."

"Still, he took their relationship far more seriously later at least," Hélissenne remarked, stroking her locks.

"Yes, later. My suspicion is that for some time Heloise was hardly foremost in his thoughts. The more he proclaims early on in their correspondence that she *never* slipped from his mind, the more you can be sure that she did."

Hélissenne stopped playing with her hair amid-stroke and looked at the inspector quizzically.

"It was not as if someone had asked him, 'Do you ever think about anything other than Heloise?' and he had answered 'Never.' Abelard repeatedly brings it up himself in the form of a negation, which is obviously the only way the thought that she had passed clear out of his mind at certain points could come to consciousness. It is basic Freud." Canal looked Hélissenne in the eye.

"Huh," she mumbled. "I guess I'm not too familiar with that sort of thing."

"Anyway, shortly after Heloise reproached him in this letter—I think it is number twenty-five in the published edition—for neglecting her and for having merely feigned love for her, not true love, he intimates that in his view nothing about their relationship was solidified as long as something was still undone, suggesting that his love for her would only become complete through intercourse. Shortly before that, he had complained to her that 'envious time looms over our love, and yet you delay as if we were at leisure,'" the inspector

125

recited from memory, and the words suddenly struck him as an adventitious precursor of Marvell's "time's winged chariot hurrying near."

"It is pretty obvious by letter twenty-nine," he continued, "when Heloise says that she has given up everything and submitted herself entirely to his rule, that she has overcome any reservations she may have had about sex before marriage and given herself over to him, soul *and* body—something Abelard could hardly have anticipated at the outset."

Seeing that Hélissenne was deep in thought, Canal added, "I thought you might be able to detect some particularly noticeable changes in his handwriting around this time—in incipit twenty-six, where I suspect he is feeling rather guilty about having neglected Heloise while fooling around with some barmaid, and in letters thirty and thirty-one where he is no doubt overjoyed about having had intercourse with Heloise and perhaps at least partially confused about where things with her are headed."

Seeing Hélissenne looking distracted, and possibly even distraught, Canal said, "I hope I have not said anything to upset you."

Hélissenne came out of her reverie and looked him in the eye. "You haven't yet had a chance to read the complete set of letters we found, have you?" she asked.

Canal shook his head.

"Strangely enough, the more complete version seems to bear out what you said—not explicitly, of course, because neither writer makes any direct reference to sex, much less to any other sexual partner, but there are even more hints here," she pointed to the parchment in front of them, "than in the extracts Jean de la Véprie copied," she pointed to Canal's published edition. The Poitevine paused for a moment, playing with her uppermost shirt button, and then went on, "I didn't really want to make anything of those hints, because they seemed too outrageous."

126

"And yet we know that they slept together at some point. Abelard even claims to have taken Heloise *nolens volens* on occasion, which she seems to have very much appreciated, if the letters she wrote him sixteen years later are to be believed, suggesting that it was more like coaxing than forcing, or that his very will to compel her thrilled her with the sensation that she had met her master." Looking Hélissenne in the eye, Canal inquired, "What exactly is it that you find hard to believe?"

"You make it sound," she replied, wondering why a retired secret serviceman would have the kind of discernment he appeared to have, "like Abelard never managed to reconcile his love for Heloise with having sexual relations with her."

"If he did, it certainly did not last very long. There seem to be quite a few ups and downs during their correspondence, and although she is overjoyed when she discovers she is pregnant, he is horrified and alights upon a course of action that makes Heloise miserable for the rest of her life. He virtually forces her to marry him in secret, even though marriage in their day and age was more about property and status than about love, and was even felt by Heloise to often be antithetical to love."

His discussant seemed to be waiting for him to get to the point—actually she was marveling at his ability to speak like he was reading from a book, so perfectly formed were his sentences at times—so the inspector went on, "She thinks marriage is, moreover, the worst thing possible for Abelard's career. And, to her mind, his career takes precedence over everything else. But as soon as they are married, he shuts her up in a convent, even though she has absolutely no interest in becoming a nun. Why, we have to ask ourselves, does he do these things?"

"So no other man will ever be able to possess her?"

"Precisely. If he could not have her—because the Church frowned upon men in his position living with their wives and, later, because her uncle castrated him for refusing to make the marriage public and thereby saving the family's reputation— Abelard was going to make damn well sure nobody else would have her either."

"Is that sort of possessiveness always part and parcel of love, in your experience?" Hélissenne asked the older man, leaning away from him a bit in her chair.

"It is not clear to me that it has any connection with love at all. Whatever love Abelard may have had for Heloise seems to have dissipated when she became pregnant. The fact that he ravished her in the convent he had sent her to, after she had given birth to their child, need not be taken as a sign of true love on *his* part. On her part, yes. For she says in her later letters that, even during Holy Mass, *she* cannot stop thinking about their wonderful sexual experiences in such illicit places as the rectory of the convent—on a holy day to boot. His remaining interest in her, however, strikes me as nothing but pure lust.

"He writes her sixteen years later, when his lust can no longer be acted upon due to emasculation, only out of guilt, only because she begs him to in the first of their famous later letters," the inspector continued, happy to air thoughts he had often had with this obviously interested girl. "Heloise still loves him with 'a love beyond measure,' and believes they could have lived and piously worshipped God together in the traditionally Old Testament way. Her choice of Abelard involved some sort of *oui insondable*, a mysterious, inexplicable YES that went to the very core of her being, and that removed him from any scale of comparison with other men. To her he was absolutely perfect—there was no question of some other, better, smarter, richer man coming along."

Canal paused for a moment, his fingers riffling through the parchment pages spread out on the table. "She even says some pretty delusional sounding things about him—that no philosopher or even king has ever been as famous as him, no songwriter or singer as accomplished, no man as sought after by flocks of women. But I think the point is that she feels he is and always will be *perfect for her*."

Hélissenne had been listening with rapt attention as Canal spoke. As she remained silent now, caressing a page of parchment, he added, "Abelard, on the other hand, appears to have fallen out of love utterly and completely by the later letters—there seems to have been no enduring, unfathomable YES on his part, or if there was, castration cut it short. To Abelard, Heloise was but the shaddock or forbidden fruit of which he tasted—not out of love, for he appears to have completely forgotten that he was ever in love with her, addressed his every waking thought to her, and even went so far once as to equate her with God, playing on the similarity of her name with that of the supreme being, Elohim. A decade and a half later he has obliterated all of that from his mind, reconceptualizing what they had as nothing but lust on his part, he having been a victim of the superficial splendor of the accursed apple.

"While she is preoccupied with the ethics of friendship that grow out of one's choice of a lover," the inspector continued, wishing to drive home one of his pet insights about the ill-fated couple, "he refuses to believe he has chosen at all—love came over him and conquered him, short-circuiting his will. He gives Heloise the advice she requests in her later letters for the running of her convent strictly because she implores him to do so in the name of their former affection. He does not do so out of any remaining *dilectio*."

"What a tragedy!" Hélissenne exclaimed almost involuntarily.

"You think of it as a tragedy?"

"Yes, I think Heloise was right to try to do whatever was best for Abelard's career."

"How do you mean?"

"She believed Abelard to be the most important thinker of her time, and felt that his intellectual career was far more important than their individual happiness."

"And you consider that to be praiseworthy?" the Frenchman asked in wonderment. "You think his posthumous life, his going down in history as a famous philosopher, was more valuable than their real lives in their own time?"

"I consider it praiseworthy," Hélissenne replied defensively, "that she adopted Abelard's ambitions as her own, and wanted for him what he himself wanted, regardless of the cost."

"Yes, it is certainly rare to find that kind of selflessness in people, especially nowadays," Canal said, examining her face acutely. "But do you not think that the cost *should* be factored in? Abelard's ambition was ruining his health—you know that some ten years earlier he had already had what today we would surely call a nervous breakdown, due it seems to over-work growing out of his unbridled ambition?"

She nodded that she did, so he went on, "And we must not forget that he was already quite famous when he and Heloise first met. She may have felt she was helping him become still more prominent, but fame has never made anyone really happy. Abelard seems to have spent many a miserable year fretting over his reputation and legacy later in life."

"So you think Heloise shouldn't have adopted her lover's ambition as her own?" Hélissenne asked, quite incredulous at the inspector's insinuation.

"If she were a nineteenth-century heroine, I would be tempted to conclude that she had deliberately placed his career above all else so as to provide their relationship with an insurmountable obstacle and deliberately turn her life into a romantic tragedy."

"And yet she is anything but a nineteenth-century heroine," Hélissenne objected indignantly.

"Precisely. So we have to wonder why she gave precedence to his ambition, giving up on her own desire to be with Abelard. Did she want her beloved to be the most eminent writer of all times so that she would be immortalized as his loved one, Dante's Beatrice before the letter? Did she mistake lowering herself for raising him up? Did she so strongly embrace submission to his will in all matters that she went along with decisions he made that could not but be disastrous for her and even for him as well? How can anyone please a man who is destroying himself, or who does not know what he wants and keeps pursuing contradictory courses of action? Was Heloise so wedded to a certain conception of a relationship between a man and a woman that she accepted choices Abelard made that ultimately rendered their relationship impossible?"

It was clear from the look on her face that the twenty-something year old had never considered such questions before. "I guess we will never know her true motives," she eventually proffered. "I have to admit that I had been thinking of her as an incredibly spiritual woman, who eventually became something of a *sainte-femme* as the abbess of the convent at the Paraclete."

"A *sainte-femme*?" Canal echoed, pondering this. "I was thinking of her as something more along the lines of a *sinthome*," he mumbled, employing the old French word for symptom, as he was wont to do, his train of thought proceeding by homonyms, *saint-homme* and *sinthome* being pronounced identically in French.

"A *saint-homme*? You were thinking of her as a holy man?"

"Far from it! There is nothing the slightest bit masculine about her, and she even expresses her wish to be taken and to be everything to a man in a way that few women over the centuries have done, thinking it unseemly. Well, few women except for those invented by romance novelists."

This seemed to resonate with Hélissenne, and she listened and reflected silently for some moments as she twirled her flowing hair.

Perceiving this, Canal went on, "Nor would I call her holy, given her comments about willingly following Abelard into Vulcan's flames if he had commanded it, and about thoughts of him interfering with her prayers, his image stealing between her and God. Unless, of course, you want to equate a man for a woman with God, and consider her devotion to him holy," he added, "which I guess is not wholly out of the question!"

"No," Hélissenne slowly stated, giving the surprised inspector the impression that she had already given the idea some thought, "I think it is not."

XXVII

R andolph Forster III was feeling pretty proud of himself for a change. Sipping a large scotch on the terrace of an out-of-the-way café in the town of Quillan, not far from Lapradelle, he surveyed the landscape, metaphorically speaking, that is. Geoffrey, that annoying Casanova from Yale, was down for the count—safely shackled and shivering at about seven thousand feet—Hélissenne was a pushover, and the letters would soon be his.

And none too soon, he reflected. His academic career had been sugarcoated on the outside and a nonstarter on the inside. He had faked and cheated his way through preparatory school, bullying the brainy kids into doing his homework for him, copying off their exams in class, and bs-ing his way through college interviews and so-called oral exams where the right attitude always stood him in good stead even when he had done little or none of the coursework. With the right connections and the proper family background, the best schools had had no choice but to accept him if they wanted to continue to receive his family's ever-so-generous donations. So what if he didn't promise to be the sharpest tool in the shed?

But graduate school had been different. An elaborate deal had had to be cut with Harvard's Department of Classics for him to be accepted. He had been granted neither a research nor a teaching fellowship, which meant that his parents were laying out something like a cool hundred grand a year for him to dally there. Although for many years they had diligently found excuse after excuse for his less than stellar performance at prep school and at Harvard as an undergraduate, they were finally beginning to tire of him accomplishing almost nothing year after year, and being repeatedly put on academic probation. They couldn't imagine such a thing happening to a Forster, three previous generations of whom had sailed effortlessly through the venerable institution of higher education.

But his parents' frustration with him was nothing compared to the pressure he now felt from the classics department itself. His parents, he knew, would always cave sooner or later—out of guilt for having neglected him virtually his entire life, or at least so he liked to tell everyone, as it seemed to garner him pity from those who had never imagined being shipped off to boarding school and leaving their cozy family home.

In reality, it was Randolph himself who at age twelve had asked to be sent to boarding school. "Why?" he wondered, looking around him at the other people drinking not nearly as heavily as himself at the nearby tables. There being no one around from whom to elicit compassion, he admitted to himself for the first time ever that it was *not* because his parents were ogres but for a reason as superficial as he was: many of his friends at their country club had enrolled in that secondary school and he didn't want to feel left out. There had been a perfectly good private school close to home that he could have attended, and indeed his parents had already secured him a place there, wanting to have more contact with their child than either of them had had with their own parents. But Randolph had thrown tantrum after tantrum until they had finally given in.

Still he preferred to portray himself to whoever would listen as having been unwanted and pushed out of the nest at a tender age, all of which served—at least in his discourse, if not in the deepest recesses of his own psyche—to excuse his current immaturity. For he had never had, he asserted, any proper adult role models to imitate, no one from whom to learn how to be a grown-up.

Even his parents, who knew full well that Randolph himself had requested to be sent away, cut him infinite slack, believing that they must have done *something* wrong to make him want to leave home in the first place. They willingly pretended to believe his excuses and they even portrayed and defended him as a sensitive child who needed understanding to his prep school headmaster and undergraduate dean when contacted about his sorely inadequate performance.

Hell, if he were kicked out of graduate school, he mused to himself while he knocked back the remaining scotch in his glass and signaled the waiter to bring another, his folks would probably blame it on themselves!

His professors, on the other hand, had become far less patient with him, and the chair of his department was manifestly on the verge of booting him out. As an undergraduate, he had quickly grasped that the ticket to keeping up appearances in his major was requesting to take incompletes in his classes. Certain of his instructors, believing this meant he was genuinely interested in the material and in doing well in their courses, but not wanting to be bothered with the extra paperwork involved or with reading leftover papers from a former course during the summer or the following year, had ended up giving him passing grades without him turning in any work at all. Others had taken the time to submit the special forms incompletes required but, when they received the garbage he eventually scraped together and put down on paper, had obviously read just one word out of five—practicing Evelyn Wood's speed-reading dynamics—somewhere between the morning paper and their drive to the supermarket and had miraculously passed him, allowing him to obtain his sheepskin.

The only reason he had gone into classics in the first place was that Latin had sunk in easily in prep school without any exertion on his part. He had no love for the subject matter and certainly had no intention to work hard at anything whatsoever—hadn't he been raised, after all, by his parents his whole life to be a privileged member of the leisure class? Graduate school might seem absurd for one in his position, but he had to do something—he certainly didn't want to get a job, perish the thought!—and the obstreperous university fraternities and clubs were just his speed. He had always done the minimum necessary in high school and college to make his teachers, well, if not happy, at least not overly ashamed of letting him advance to the next level.

But they were not so forgiving in his graduate program. Certain professors in the classics department had already known him as an undergraduate and knew of his parents' generous contributions to the school, but they were determined to hold the line when it came to minting Ph.Ds. They were expecting him to work, and the eight incompletes he had racked up prior to beginning his third year of the graduate program—a record by any standards—were not going to disappear without him producing something.

A miracle find of some kind just might do the trick, he had thought when signing up for the internship in the Pyrenees, but the gamble thus far had not paid off. He had spent the whole summer digging and found only fool's gold—no original topic for his dissertation and no fabulous discovery with which to negotiate. Whether the find were of scholarly interest or simply a prestigious archeological artifact to donate to Harvard's stuffy collections, Randolph couldn't have cared less. Indeed, if he had his druthers, he'd prefer there be no work at all involved for him other than negotiating the donation in exchange for a few overlooked I-grades.

"Let one of those grey-haired, bespectacled bookworms slog through the musty old letters and write a scholarly monograph

136

on them," he exclaimed to himself with relish, starting on the new glass of his favorite scotch that the waiter had just set down before him. This was the life for him, he felt, stretching his legs out under the table and feeling the warm sun on his skin. That sort of work was for the birds!

But somber reflections soon disturbed Randolph's unruffled feeling of well-being. As if his academic situation weren't dire enough, his social life too had recently begun to come apart at the seams. Muffy, his Vassar-educated girlfriend of three years, had finally stopped believing his stories about his accomplishments and exploits. The tales he told her had become so complicated that he himself could no longer recall all their inventive details and she had eventually caught him out in so many blatant contradictions that she had broken it off in exasperation, despite being enamored of his parents and family connections.

Sitting there on the terrace, deep in his cups, he admitted to himself that he had told so many different stories to people over the years opportunistically—to procure their pity, get let off the hook by them, or work his way into bed with them—that he was no longer sure where the truth lay on myriad subjects. Had he been sexually abused by his parents or relatives? Probably not, he reflected, taking another long swig of the eighty proof, even if he had led a number of people to believe it, including his departmental advisor. Had he been beaten as a child by his father or grandfather? Spanked once or twice maybe, like everyone else, but could he recall a single real incident of anything involving so much as a paddle or a belt, much less a fist? Try as he might to scan his memory banks, the search yielded nada, niente, bupkis. Drinking had been helping him, he felt, forget how much he'd forgotten about things that had never actually happened ...

He had been mistreated by love, he had told Muffy again and again to win her sympathy, led on by and misled by girls. The truth was simply that he had never had much luck with girls, a failing he blithely chalked up to being shipped off to an all boys preparatory school—okay, so not exactly "shipped off." Still, if he couldn't talk to girls, it was obviously his parents' fault for not having given him any sisters. Had he had sisters like some of his other friends, he'd certainly have been comfortable around females and far more successful in wooing them.

He had hoped that the archeological internship would bring him into close proximity with a bevy of pretty French girls dying to get to know a rich American—and weren't all Americans rich to the French? But instead of fostering fascination, his familiarity with them had bred contempt. None of the French females found him the least bit seductive or intriguing—well, maybe Isabeau had at the outset, but it hadn't lasted very long—and most of them gave him a wide berth.

For a while, Randolph had managed to chalk up their disdain for him to their recent scorn for all Americans in the aftermath of the Iraq war. But Geoffrey's success with Hélissenne—the most delectable girl Randolph had met in a long time and the only one at the dig of noble descent from what he had heard—not to mention the Yalie's easy friendship with Isabeau, the next prettiest number, had made it hard for Randolph to go on believing his own excuse. That irked him even more than his own lack of success.

He had resorted to befriending the English-speaking girls among the interns, even though they had no cachet for him and he wasn't attracted to any of them. At least they seemed to like the sauce as much as he did, which was more and more all the time.

Overhearing snatches of Hélissenne and Geoffrey's conversation at the café the prior Saturday, he was overjoyed at the possibility of killing three birds with one stone: an important find might go a long way toward improving his academic standing, Geoffrey would be humiliated, and Hélissenne—who had listened to him politely the first few days of the internship but had rebuffed him ever since as if he were one of the hoi polloi, or worse still, the lowest of the low, instead of a blue blood like herself—would be at his mercy!

It wasn't that Randolph found Hélissenne irresistibly attractive, for she wasn't the blond-and-blue-eyed type he usually lusted after, or that he thought her personality captivating. It was just that he imagined he would look good being seen with her, she being a paragon of feminine pulchritude. He savored this last word, finding it ugly and harsh, which was, he felt fitting, feminine loveliness having tremendous power over him, which he resented enormously. When he saw a gorgeous woman, his whole day would be ruined because he could think of nothing else and yet could not have her. That made him want to smash female beauty, mangle it, destroy it!

But an American in France was supposed to have flings with French girls, the sexiest and most desirable on the planet according to what he'd always heard, and he wanted to be able to show pictures of her to his buddies back in Cambridge. He reveled in the thought of making them feel inadequate for never having been able to date such an attractive girl as him, and enjoyed anticipating the reaction of the aristocratic girls he knew, whom he hoped would feel taken down a notch as they compared themselves unfavorably to Hélissenne's classic features and poised beauty. There was nothing he liked better than taking girls down a peg, knocking them off the pedestal he felt they put themselves on, thinking they were better than him, or at least could *do* better than him.

Building himself up meant knocking them down—so what of it? If he couldn't truly win a girl over, he might as well be like Lord Byron, "mad, bad, and dangerous to know."

Hélissenne would be forced to pose for whatever pictures he wanted and as many as he wanted, and he would derive great pleasure from making up salacious, ego-boosting stories about her to his friends back home. He had her right where he wanted her.

And boy would she and her Yalie be surprised by what he had up his sleeve! He polished off his fourth scotch and licked his lips in eager anticipation of what was to follow.

XXVIII

Day was just beginning to break when the disguised Inspector Canal started up the trail from a small dirt parking lot ten miles from the Cabane de la Balmette. He had switched cars with Hélissenne just in case Randolph knew the make and model of Geoffrey's car and planned to ambush her long before she got to the refuge. She was to set out about an hour and a half later from a different trailhead so they could not be suspected of being fellow travelers. Picking his way among the aspen-like birches and pines, he replayed the conversation he had had with Hélissenne over dinner the night before and pondered the likelihood of anyone in the younger generations making a relationship work.

When, after they had discussed at some length the common divergence of love and sexual desire among men and its probable Oedipal causes, the inspector had asked the young Poitevine how she saw the future, she had replied, "I haven't really given it much thought, I have to admit. Some of my friends have been planning out an academic or curator career since they got to college, but I've always just followed my own interests and figure I'll just keep pursuing them wherever they happen to lead. So far they've led me to what people so glibly call the dark ages—it fascinates me how people lived at that time! I don't see anything particularly dark about them."

She had made it clear that she didn't work at her studies so much because she believed in the virtue of hard work or was trying to get into the good graces of a professor who could help her move up the proverbial ladder, but simply because she was truly engrossed in what she did. Regarding the years to come, she had added, "I always felt I'd someday meet someone who shared my passions, someone like Geoffrey, maybe."

"Geoffrey shares your passions?" Canal had asked.

"At least some of them," she had replied, "and far more of them than most other people I've met. I think he's less interested in archeology per se than I am, although finding those letters may have changed that a bit."

"Yes, I think you are right," the inspector had said, laughing.

"So he can be a professor somewhere," she had proposed, as if she had given it some prior thought, "and we can spend our summers digging around beautiful spots like Puilaurens."

"Not a bad plan," Canal had commented. "But what if he only gets a job in Kalamazoo or Podunk?"

"Kalamawhat?" she had asked, trying to repeat at least part of the first sound Canal had produced.

"They are small college towns in America, out in the middle of nowhere."

"That'll be just fine with me, as long as I'm with my Geoffrey."

"And what if he is unhappy there, feeling it is not good enough for him?"

"Well, then, I'll just have to find a way to make him realize he's leading the good life with me wherever we are. Career isn't everything—even for him!" she had replied, winking at Canal in reference to their conversation earlier that day, suggesting that at least some of what he'd said about Abelard and Heloise's fruitless choices had struck a chord.

In response to his encouraging "Well said! I see you have got it all worked out," Hélissenne had gone on, "But as Heloise says, love requires constant faithful effort—'the services of true love are continually owed.' It isn't enough to think once of doing something that manifests one's love, or even say one will do it, for it to be so. It requires a never-ending series of small loving gestures and concessions, putting oneself aside for two."

"Yes," Canal had agreed heartily, "for two and not just for one. We must not delude ourselves, like Abelard with his 'love makes two souls the same *indifferenter*, without difference,' into thinking that two can become one." Such so-called indifference theories might have been promoted by theologians to explain the Trinity, Canal had reflected, but they had no plausible place in discussions of love.

The conversation had made the inspector realize that Hélissenne was the only girl he had encountered in ages who *openly* aspired to be what so many other women secretly aspired to be—taken and wholly possessed by a man, *sa chose*. At least it was the *hidden* aspiration of most of the women of his own generation and of the younger generation as well, he suspected. Virtually all the other younger women he had met in recent years were loath to admit any such desire until years and years into an analysis.

"Pas de retraite anticipée pour les analystes," he mused, and smiled at his own unintended quasi-double entendre. Indeed, there was no point, he reflected, in analysts eagerly anticipating retirement, much less early retirement, given how much work would be required to undo the years of ideology, brainwashing, television … Girls were now taught to be, or told they should be, just like boys, wanting all the same things as boys, in order to supply ever more workers to the economic machine, which preferred perfectly generic or universal producers: raceless, sexless, faithless, and rootless.

It had already been hard enough, the inspector felt as he arrived at one of the steeper parts of the trail, when sex roles at least supplemented each other. They could never truly complement each other, men and women forever looking for different things from each other and missing each other in ineluctable ways, but times now struck him as tougher still. Did men really want the women they were involved with to be so independent they could do everything on their own with no help from men? The inspector found that hard to believe, except maybe on the part of men who avoided commitment like the plague, equating all women who appeared to need something with their mothers who they felt they had a duty to assist.

Did women really go for men who want them to be self-sufficient, needing little if anything from men? Nothing Canal had ever heard behind closed doors confirmed any such thing except from women who were running away from men either to punish their fathers or to confirm their mothers' beliefs that all men were unreliable liars and cheaters. Or, maybe even more commonly, to comply with their mothers' ferocious prohibitions against their daughters having *any* men of their own! If so many boys came to the erroneous conclusion by age five that *all* girls were off-limits, not just mom, perhaps nearly as many girls came to the conclusion that *all* boys were off-limits. "Has anyone," he asked himself, "ever written about the mother, not of the primal horde, but who nevertheless keeps all the men to herself—the kind that has to have the undivided attention of every male that comes within her orbit, allowing her daughter none?"

Hélissenne, at least, was certainly not in the category of women who consciously believed they should not need anything from a man, and she didn't even have a decade or so of analysis under her belt. Resting for a moment alongside the rocky trail, Canal wondered how such a feat had been possible.

Maybe she and Geoffrey had a chance, after all. It would all depend, he told himself, on Geoffrey's willingness to change, to come to grips with his ambition and get over the residual

Oedipal struggles that were likely keeping love and sexual desire so separate for him. Would he be able and willing to deal with a woman who explicitly wished to be everything for him? Could he handle that? Could he even want it? Or would he be scared off by it, Canal asked himself, like so many others who were interested only in the chase, interested only in women who were running away from them, not toward them?

XXIX

Lost in such matinal reflections a couple of miles up the trail, Canal did not hear the whistling sound coming from off to his left until it had occurred several times. Peering into the dark woods down the slope, Canal eventually glimpsed a head peering out from behind a tree.

"Inspector Canal?" it whispered.

"Yes," he replied uncertainly.

"It's me, Geoffrey."

"Geoffrey?" the Frenchman cried. Then, recognizing Geoffrey's tousled hair and square jaw in the deep shade of the pines, Canal exclaimed, "Geoffrey, my boy, how did you get away?"

Still trying to talk softly, the American excitedly recited his tale as though he had been rehearsing in his mind what he would say for some time already. "The refuge Randolph's goons tied me up in was disgustingly dirty and I managed to find plenty of broken glass to work with. It must have taken me a few hours to cut the ropes on my hands and feet—my fingers are all bloody—but I finally managed to get free. Then I had to cut the rope on the door, and it was none too soon—it was freezing up there!"

"Why do you not come out from behind the tree onto the trail where I can hear you better?"

"I'm naked," Geoffrey explained sheepishly in a still more hushed tone of voice. "They took all my clothes!"

"Well there is no need to be embarrassed for my sake," Canal said, smiling and walking down the slope toward the tree where Geoffrey was, even as he puzzled over Randolph's motives for inflicting such harsh treatment. "I have probably got something you can put on here." Drawing closer he saw that Geoffrey was barefoot and that his feet were caked with blood and dirt. "They took your shoes too?"

"Yes, that was the cruelest part, those bastards! Walking on the trail in the dark at least helped me warm up a little bit, but my feet are killing me."

"Here, put these on," said the inspector, extracting a sweater and sweatpants from his rucksack. "Luckily I always bring extra layers for the higher elevations." Geoffrey dressed quickly, even though the clothes were a bit too small for his frame.

"Now let us get your feet cleaned up," Canal directed. He sat the American down on a fallen fir, produced a bottle of water, and washed his feet and hands off at some length. He put Band-Aids from his first-aid kit on only the worst cuts on his soles, not having nearly enough dressings for all his wounds. Next he gave Geoffrey the extra pair of socks he always brought along with him when he hiked, and gloves for his lacerated hands. Realizing that they were still a couple of miles from the trailhead, and that Geoffrey was far too heavy for Canal to carry all that way, Canal took out a pocket knife and began, despite Geoffrey's protestations, cutting large patches out of the back of the lined leather jacket he had been wearing to fashion primitive moccasins for Geoffrey, having no second pair of shoes to offer.

The American would be eternally grateful.

"What a relief!" Geoffrey exclaimed as Canal finished tying the leather strips onto the boy's oversized feet with some spare shoe laces. "I'm so glad it was you and not Hélissenne I ran into first. It would have been awfully embarrassing, encountering her naked and looking like a wreck!"

"Encountering her naked?" Canal repeated as they stood up and set off back down the trail, hearing that the nakedness in the formulation could be on either side, "You had time to be concerned about that?"

"Well, it was pretty humiliating, what they did to me—in fact it was one fright after another."

"How do you mean?"

"Well, first they took me to a different refuge than the Cabane de la Balmette, one a couple of miles past the agreed upon exchange site. That's when I realized they intended to mess with Hélissenne's head and not make an even exchange as they had said they would. Then, rather than just lock me up for the night with a sleeping bag and a loaf of bread, which would have at least been humane, they stripped off all my clothes, bound me hand and foot, and left me to starve and freeze!"

Canal could tell from Geoffrey's indignant tone of voice that the young man had been through a true ordeal.

"But the worst thing of all," Geoffrey went on, "was the way they hung around holding their big hunting knives after tying me up naked. I couldn't stop thinking they were going to sever me asunder, castrate me, just like Heloise's uncle did to Abelard! It suddenly struck me that our situations were eerily parallel—Hélissenne, like Heloise, was born in Fontevrault, barely knew her parents, was home schooled by a private tutor, and raised for the past twenty years by her uncle."

"Lots of children are raised by their relatives," Canal commented, and before Geoffrey could go on, he directed him away from the main trail, down a footpath off to their left.

"Why are you changing trails? Isn't your car parked at the bottom of this one?"

"Actually *your* car is," Canal explained. "Hélissenne took my car and will be heading up this other trail shortly, if she has not already started," he added, glancing at his watch and calculating in his head. "We decided to come separately, by different trails, and about an hour and a half apart so they would not imagine for a moment that we were working together."

"Good thinking."

"We want to make sure Hélissenne does not venture up the trail all by herself now when there is no need to take any further risks."

"Right." Proceeding down the path, Geoffrey picked up the thread. "Like I was saying, I couldn't get over the similarities between Abelard's situation and my own. Lying there on the ground, watching those two guys brandishing their huge knives, I remembered that Hélissenne told me her uncle, a rather forbidding man apparently, is none too happy with the idea of her dating an American graduate student. I started imagining that her uncle was somehow in cahoots with Randolph, and that he'd found out that Hélissenne and I had slept together. Her uncle's name, Filbert, is even almost identical to that of Heloise's uncle Fulbert—it's uncanny!"

"I suspect that you and Abelard have a lot less in common than you think."

"Well that sure didn't stop me from imagining all kinds of harrowing things! I was seriously starting to panic before I saw them finally use their knives to cut some more rope—it must've been what they locked the cabin door with, as if they hadn't already tied me up well enough."

"The fact that you are here right now proves they had not."

"I guess not," the American conceded. "I wondered if Randolph had told his henchmen to spend the night up there with me, and they figured they could dispense with freezing their butts off by just locking me in thoroughly."

150

"Well, if you are right, they are probably on their way back up the trail right now, so we should keep it down a little and keep an eye out for them."

"Okay," Geoffrey whispered, "but I don't think they know about this other trail—they dragged me up the main one, for whatever that's worth."

XXX

Geoffrey thanked his stars that his feet went completely numb again after a mile of such unusual treatment and his thoughts turned to something other than physical pain. After the two men had been silent for some time, he spoke anew to the inspector, albeit softly.

"You know, I couldn't help thinking, while I was working away endlessly at the ropes with those shards of glass, that if only I'd been a genius or had a Green Beret's bravery I'd have been able to find some other way out of this mess."

"Bravery?"

"Yes, you see, there was this point while they were shoving me up the trail yesterday at which I started thinking, if I just pretended to have sprained my ankle, they'd have to more or less carry me, one on either side, and I could bang their heads together—like you see people do on TV."

Canal raised his eyebrows at this, but as Geoffrey was walking behind him, he noticed nothing and went on. "There was even one part of the trail higher up where the path follows a very narrow crest, the ground falling off steeply to each side, and I started thinking I could push one guy off to one side and the other off to the other." He paused for a moment, looked down, and finally added, "But then, like a coward, I started thinking my chances of remaining in the middle while both of them were trying to hold onto me wouldn't be so great and I gave that idea up."

"Which may have been the smartest thing to do, in any case."

"Maybe. But painstakingly cutting through each fiber of each damn rope there in the cabin, I started reproaching myself for not having jumped down one of the steep rock slides myself to get away from them before they had a chance to tie me up and humiliate me like that."

"*That* might have been even more dangerous," quipped Canal. "And then they would have known you had gotten away and would have either come after you or tried yet another plan—like going after Hélissenne again, but not letting go this time."

"I hadn't thought of that," Geoffrey said, slowly. Then he added, "You see, if I were a lot more intelligent, I'd have been able to think through the different possibilities better and faster."

"No, it is rather that, like so many deluded souls, you are confused about the nature of intelligence."

"Well, if I had a genius IQ—"

"*Belle jambe!*"

"Huh?"

"A lot of good it would do you," translated the inspector.

"You don't think it would do me any good? Think how much more I would know, and how much faster I would learn!"

"What are you in such a hurry to do that you need to learn faster than you already can?"

Geoffrey had drawn up alongside the Frenchman at this point on a wider section of the trail and his face evinced perplexity. "I don't know," he mumbled. "Everything—I'd like to be able to learn everything faster, so I'd know more."

"What is this obsession of yours with knowing? You need to know what you want, not a slew of facts."

154

"What I want?"

"Plenty of people with high IQs and tons of facts at their fingertips never do anything worthwhile, whether worthwhile to themselves or others, because they do not know what they want. And plenty of people who would never achieve genius scores on silly IQ tests come up with all kinds of things that please others and themselves as well—because they really get into them, genuinely pursue them, truly work at them."

"But I do know what I want," insisted Geoffrey. "At least school-wise."

"Do you?"

"I think so."

"Well, then, maybe you are more like Abelard than I thought—you know what you want academically but when it comes to your personal life ..."

"What about my personal life?" Geoffrey asked somewhat testily.

"Maybe you are not so sure what you want there?"

"No, I think it's clearer to me now. Even if I have to resolve certain conflicts in my own mind, I am in love with Hélissenne and want to make things work with her."

"So what led you to leave the hotel yesterday morning?"

"Leave the hotel?" Geoffrey asked, flummoxed.

"Yes, one can but wonder why you left the hotel without Hélissenne after your first night together. Were you not fleeing from her?"

Geoffrey stopped walking and gave the inspector a quizzical look.

"And was it not this flight from her that got you into this mess?" Canal continued, pointing to his feet and hands. "First, you wanted to spend the night with her, rather than do the cautious thing and leave town immediately, and then you regretted it or needed to escape?"

"Not at all," Geoffrey exclaimed, now that he had caught Canal's drift. "I had bought her a little gift Monday morning, just before finding out she had disappeared, and never had a chance to give it to her. I woke up early yesterday and, lying in bed, I suddenly remembered it was still in the trunk. So while she was sleeping I went down to get it for her."

"A gift?"

"Yes, a gift. Why would you imagine anything else?"

"It is not so much me as Hélissenne who must have wondered what could have possibly led you to leave the bed, much less the room."

It suddenly dawned on Geoffrey what Hélissenne had perhaps been wondering and feeling when he was not there next to her when she awoke and never returned. "Oh man!" he cried. "I forgot she couldn't have known I had bought her a pair of earrings. She must think I'm a real jerk."

Canal shook his head and reassured him, "I think she gives you more credit than that, but it cannot have failed to give her pause for thought."

"She must be furious at me, even as she's doing everything to try to get me back from Randolph and his assassins."

"I suspect it is nothing you cannot work out," Canal said reassuringly. "Especially if they are nice earrings," he added to lighten the somber turn the boy's tone had taken.

"Oh, they are! At least *I* think they are. Hopefully she will too."

Canal nodded, and then, taking Geoffrey by the elbow, guided him to continue their course down the trail, where they were hoping to encounter Hélissenne soon.

They walked in silence for a few minutes, and then Geoffrey, whose thoughts had obviously returned to their earlier topic of conversation, asked Canal quietly, "So you had been thinking I'm not very much like Abelard?"

"I think you are less like Abelard than Hélissenne is like Heloise, even if you do have a very fertile imagination for paranoid scenes like he seems to have had."

"Oh," Geoffrey said. Then, coming to the real reason behind his question, he added, "So you think Hélissenne is as smart as Heloise but I'm not as smart as Abelard."

"Few people are," Canal replied unabashedly. "Abelard was a very sharp fellow and knew a great deal of what there was to know in his era."

"So you agree I don't know that much, after all," Geoffrey goaded him, trying to get him to reveal the judgments he was sure the inspector had formed of him.

"Abelard never seems to have figured out what he wanted. He did not want to build a life with Heloise but wanted to make mad, passionate love to her now and then. He no doubt got a kick out of betraying her uncle Fulbert, as if he were stealing pleasure from a father figure right under his very nose, in some kind of Oedipal struggle. To deceive Fulbert all the better, he apparently even beat Heloise a little bit, like masters often beat their pupils at the time, to make it sound to her uncle like he was giving Heloise a serious education. It was as if Abelard needed someone to embody the law for him so he could enjoy sinning, so he could get off on feeling he was doing something filthy and prohibited." Canal glanced at Geoffrey's face. "And later he got a kick out of making love to Heloise in the very convent in which he had shut her up, ravishing her from the Almighty himself. Maybe he got a bigger kick out of imagining he was ripping God off than out of taking her!"

Geoffrey remained silent, digesting this, so Canal went on, "In any case, Abelard neither wanted to keep Heloise around nor to let her belong to anyone else. *You* at least have a chance, perhaps, of figuring out what you want from Hélissenne, instead of pushing and pulling, or rushing in contradictory directions at the same time."

"I *can* change, can't I?" Geoffrey asked the Frenchman imploringly. "People get better as they get older, don't they?"

"If they do a serious psychoanalysis, they may have a chance to. Most others just get worse."

"They get worse?" Geoffrey inquired, stunned.

"People are not like certain wines or fine musical instruments that improve with age," Canal explained, shaking his head. "Human problems rarely work themselves out by themselves. Most people's worst features simply get accentuated with the passage of time."

"I worry that I'm somehow fated to be like Abelard, and to repeat all his mistakes. You know that thing you said about him being more interested in stealing Heloise away from her protective uncle than in Heloise herself? Well, I can see that sort of thing in myself."

Canal remained silent, giving the boy a chance to speak his piece.

"Even if I managed to escape emasculation last night, I still feel I deserve it somehow for not being a constant lover. Just like Abelard, I try to lose myself in a woman, to escape from something through love, instead of trying to find myself in love like Hélissenne does. And I vacillate so much between love and resentment."

Canal drew up alongside the boy again and eyed him closely. "You never repeat what you think you are going to repeat, and you do not repeat somebody else's past, but your own," he remarked. "You repeat only what you never think there is any danger you will repeat or what you never imagine repeating, because you never even noticed it in ze first place. It is what you do not notice, because you do not want to know anything about it, that ends up running your life."

XXXI

Geoffrey was about to ask Canal what that was supposed to mean when the latter gestured to the empty parking lot at the trailhead below.

The car wasn't there. They had followed the whole trail Hélissenne was supposed to take, so they couldn't have missed her. What could have prevented her from coming?

Geoffrey required a few moments to shift gears from his earlier train of thought, but eventually suggested that perhaps the inspector and she had gotten their signals crossed and she had taken a different trail.

Canal considered the possibility for a moment, but indicated that he was convinced she knew exactly which one he had been talking about, especially since it was the only other trail on that side of the mountain. Stroking his chin, from which he had just removed the fake beard, he added, "I suppose she could have overslept, but I would have imagined she barely slept at all."

"Maybe your car broke down while she was on the way here," Geoffrey proposed calmly, not yet as alarmed as the Frenchman seemed to be.

"In that case we should run into her on the way back. I am afraid, however, that this is going to add a couple of extra miles on foot for you, unless you want to wait here while I go retrieve your car from the other trailhead."

"Wait here for Randolph and his thugs to find me again? No way! I'm coming with you."

As they set off down the road, Geoffrey turned to the inspector and began, thinking aloud, "You don't think, do you, that all of this could be some kind of ruse to … to get me out of the way so they could kidnap Hélissenne again?"

XXXII

Geoffrey visually scoured every ditch and ravine during the first tense minutes of their long drive back to Gincla, half-expecting to discover that Canal's car, with Hélissenne at the wheel, had gone off the road at every turn. He had convinced himself that Randolph was determined not merely to extort the letters from him but to steal Hélissenne away from him too, dead or alive. Perhaps Randolph had figured out which car Hélissenne would be driving and had loosened the steering column, drained the brake fluid, or partially punctured the tires. It would be child's play after that for him to simply follow her car and remove the letters once she crashed.

Geoffrey spotted a car all right, but it was *on* the road and it wasn't Canal's car. His first reaction was to duck down in the passenger seat.

"What's wrong?" the inspector asked him.

"That dark sedan that just passed in the opposite direction—that was Randolph and his henchmen!"

"Are you sure?" queried the Frenchman, trying to catch a glimpse of the car in his rearview mirror.

"Oh yes, I'll never forget the faces of those goons. I hope they didn't see me!"

"We should have anticipated that," Canal said, reflecting retroactively. He turned the car into a small dirt road hidden by some trees and positioned it so they could pull back out again quickly if need be. "If they did recognize you," he opined, "they should be turning around any second—we will wait here and see if they go by."

Geoffrey sat back up in his seat and scrutinized the few cars that went by. "Whew!" he uttered after a couple of minutes. "They must not have seen me."

"At least they will be out of the way for quite a few hours." Canal turned the key in the ignition and pulled back out onto the road in the direction of Gincla. "All we have to do now is pick up Hélissenne and leave the area. I will keep an eye out for my car—otherwise, I am sure we will find her back at the hotel. She must have been unable to leave on time for some reason."

This seemed to mollify Geoffrey, who seemed not to be thinking too clearly after his all-nighter, and Canal abstained from voicing his concerns about another possibility—that she had indeed gone to the wrong trailhead and would somehow make her way up to the Cabane de la Balmette anyway, though probably hours after the appointed time. If she were to arrive there alone with the letters, and Randolph and his acolytes were still there, they would be sure to take full advantage of the situation. Had they had two cars, Canal would have been inclined to go search for Hélissenne himself, letting Geoffrey look for her at the hotel, even though he was convinced she had known which trail she was supposed to go to, at least as of the night before. Perhaps she had misplaced the map, missed one of the turns, or simply lost her head and stopped at the first trail parking lot she came across. There would be an awful lot of them to check. As long as she was not accounted for, there was a slight chance she would fall into Randolph's hands.

Still, they did not have two cars and his co-pilot seemed to be in no condition to drive. Moreover, he was pretty sure they

162

would meet her en route or find her back at the hotel. Perhaps his solenoid had given out again, even though he had replaced it not two months earlier.

Canal suddenly realized that he himself must not have been thinking too clearly, having awoken so much earlier than usual. Why did he not simply call the hotel to see if Hélissenne were still there? All he needed to do was find a phone booth. Glancing at the map, he noted that they were still some fifteen kilometers from the next small village and who knew if the phone booth there would be in working condition? Did he even have one of those infernal magnetic cards needed to operate public phones in France? He rummaged around in his pockets and came up empty-handed. This was one of those rare times, he reflected, when a cell phone would come in handy. If Geoffrey had had one, it had obviously disappeared with his clothing.

XXXIII

The inspector maintained a pensive silence during the next part of the trip back to Gincla, keeping his eyes peeled for his car with Hélissenne at the wheel and for a phone booth.

The American, who had been up all night cutting ropes and walking down a rocky trail, slumped back into the passenger seat, his eyes closing of their own accord. Images presented themselves to Geoffrey one after another, and snatches of conversation ran through his head, words barely recognized pronounced by voices long since heard. It seemed to Geoffrey's dim consciousness that the voices were trying to tell him something, but he was too tired to focus, too sleepy to grab hold of anything.

He awoke some half an hour later to the sound of a woman's voice repeating the word *vows* over and over again. Opening his eyes, he looked all around him for the author of the voice, but became disoriented, finding no one anywhere near him other than Canal. But seeing the by now familiar forms of the Pyrenees, he soon came back to himself, as it were, remembering who he was because of where he was. Yet he could not stop himself from pronouncing aloud the word his short but refreshing sleep had thrust upon him.

"*Comment?*" the Frenchman responded involuntarily, not having noticed that the American had awoken. "Come again?"

"Oh, nothing. Just some word that drifted through my mind while my eyes were closed."

"Those are the most important kind. What was it?"

"Vows. Like wedding vows, I guess."

"Wedding vows … Does that bring anything to mind?" the inspector asked, all the while keeping two very attentive eyes on the hairpin turns he was navigating.

Geoffrey reflected groggily, bracing himself against the dashboard as the car swerved back and forth with each turn. "Seems like people make a big deal out of writing personalized wedding vows these days."

The driver confined his remarks to a barely audible grunt suggesting that he was listening.

"I guess girls go for that sort of thing more than guys do," the passenger added. "People don't seem to much like the old-fashioned vows, 'to honor and to obey,' 'to have and to hold,' and all that jazz anymore. I'm sure my parents never bothered writing special vows of their own."

"*Your* parents?"

"Yeah, in their day people just said 'I do' after the usual 'loving and cherishing' stuff the preacher would say. But it doesn't seem to matter how many newfangled vows couples come up with now to prove how strong their bond with each other is—they have just as many problems as my parents and their friends did, and get divorced even more often."

"Problems?"

"Yeah, I mean," Geoffrey fidgeted a bit in his seat, "I figure they must've had problems."

"You are not sure?"

"Not terribly, I guess. My parents were pretty private about things. They'd only argue behind closed doors after we kids were in bed." The classicist rubbed his eyes for a few moments and added, "I think something happened when I was real young." He yawned, as if profoundly uninterested in the topic.

"Something?" The display of indifference made Canal's ears perk up.

Geoffrey stretched his limbs. "My father was away for a while," he eventually said, yawning again. "It must've been not long after my sister was born."

"Where was he?"

"I never figured that out. For a long time I believed he had gone into the military, but later in school I learned there weren't any wars being fought at that time. And when I finally asked my father, he told me he would have declared himself a conscientious objector if the government had ever tried to draft him."

"So you were alone with your mother for some time?"

"Yeah. But I'm not sure for how long. I was probably around three or four."

"She never told you where your father was?"

"She did tell me, but she used some word that I thought was *military*, but I was obviously mistaken. It was something like mala or mana ... with terry at the end."

"Sounds like mandatory, but that does not make any sense. Or monetary, but that is hardly a place."

"No," Geoffrey said slowly, and then it hit him. "Monastery. It must have been monastery," he exclaimed.

"Monastery?"

"Yes." Reflecting for a few moments, Geoffrey added, "That would explain a lot of things. He must have gone off to a monastery but in the end never took his vows."

"Unless he broke them."

"I doubt that. He isn't the kind of man to break a promise." After a few short moments, he amended, "Though I guess he seriously contemplated breaking his promise to my mother."

"Your father is a religious man?"

"Religious, I'm not so sure. But he is ascetic, very uptight about his body and nakedness, and a real prude when it comes to sexual subjects."

Canal raised his eyebrows at this, but his facial gesture was lost on Geoffrey who had just detected the little sign indicating that they had arrived at Gincla, meaning that the hotel Hélissenne was to have set forth from would be right around the corner.

XXXIV

The inspector's car was nowhere to be seen in the hotel parking lot and the hotel itself was in an uproar when the two men arrived. Several of the staff and a number of the guests, many of them dressed only in their bathrobes and slippers, were talking excitedly and simultaneously in the reception area to two police officers who seemed to have arrived just moments before.

While the gendarmes tried to figure out who to listen to, Canal took Madame Cochenille by the arm and steered her outside. At first she snapped at him for taking her away from the main theater of activity, for it was her wont to automatically snap at everyone, whether friend or foe, and then assess the situation at her leisure, becoming gentle and helpful if she so pleased, blithely assuming that no one would ever hold her initially prickly reaction against her. Recalling her interest in the handsome and apparently well-to-do inspector, which had been growing over the past few days, she became conciliatory and willingly followed him out onto the patio where Geoffrey was waiting.

In response to his query, she explained that she had over-slept for the first time in ages and had been awoken by loud noises coming from the reception area shortly before eight. By the time she had dressed and made it downstairs, no one was there. The front door was open and she heard a car, but could see nothing. Her first assumption had been that the restaurant's hugely expensive silver service had been stolen, so she had raced to the dining room and back kitchen, but all was as she had left it the night before. Coming back into the reception area, she had checked the petty cash drawer, but it had not been touched either. Stumped, she had finally sat down at the desk at which she did the books, and for the first time had felt as if something were missing.

Turning to her left, she had discovered a gaping hole in the wall where the safe had been. Having been unable to crack the safe, the thieves had simply taken the whole thing with them. "Those scoundrels!" she cried. "When I catch them, I'll, well I'll …," she trailed off, not knowing how to finish her threat in a ladylike manner.

The two listeners expressed astonishment at her tale.

"But we saw Randolph and his men a full hour's drive from here right around eight-thirty," exclaimed Canal. "They could not have stolen the safe and gotten that far away that quickly—somebody else must have stolen the safe."

"Maybe Randolph has other people working for him too," Geoffrey suggested.

Canal considered this. "But if he were the one who sent the thieves here, why would he be heading to the Cabane de la Balmette? He would already have what he wants."

"Unless his goal is to capture Hélissenne too," Geoffrey opined, giving Canal a meaningful look.

"If he wanted both the letters *and* the girl, he could have simply waited for Hélissenne to deliver them and herself to him in the mountains on a silver platter. You were a spent force, as far as he knew, and would be unable to intervene since you were supposedly bound and gagged at a different location. There was no need for him to take extra risks," the Frenchman insisted. "No, there must be somebody else involved." Turning to the hotel owner, Canal was about to ask a question when Geoffrey beat him to the punch.

"Have you seen Hélissenne?" he cried.

Madame Cochenille had obviously forgotten all about Hélissenne, for it suddenly occurred to her that she had been supposed to do something—just what it was had slipped her mind. The flood of hotel guests into the reception area in the course of the morning to find out what all the hubbub was about had wiped everything else out of her head, and she only now realized that there had been no sign of the Poitevine.

Noting the boy's worry, Canal told Geoffrey that, despite not having the letters, Hélissenne had no doubt wanted to show up at the Cabane de la Balmette to find Geoffrey and explain the situation to the kidnappers. She must have taken a wrong turn or gone to the wrong trailhead, as the student had conjectured, and would eventually figure that out and return safely to the hotel. To himself, Canal admitted another possibility—that the thieves had arrived just as Hélissenne had entered the reception area and that they had taken her and Canal's car with them—but he saw no reason to alarm the boy with thoughts of such a remote eventuality, since she was to have left the hotel closer to six-thirty than to eight.

The inspector glanced at his watch and stroked his chin. "Whoever they are, they have about an hour-and-a-half head start on us," he began. "Which way did the car seem to you to go?" he asked Mme. Cochenille.

"Toward the valley." The hotelier pointed her finger in the direction opposite the Pyrenees. "Definitely toward the valley."

"Definitely?" Canal asked, concerned. "Why did you repeat yourself if you are sure?"

"I was just repassing the scene in my head."

"Good," Canal said encouragingly. "Cast your mind back to the scene again and try to listen to that car you heard. What did it sound like?"

"*J'sais pas*," she mumbled, garbling in typical French fashion her "I don't know" response. "Like an ordinary car," she added, shrugging her shoulders.

"Try to recall the sound of the motor. Was it a deep, full-throated motor sound? The kind of pulsating sound a diesel motor makes? Or a high-pitched tone?"

"High-pitched," she replied smiling, happy to remember this particular detail for the inspector who for once was paying her so much attention. "In fact, very high-pitched, almost like a motorcycle."

"Any squealing of tires or skidding on gravel?"

"No, I didn't hear anything like that."

"What about shifting of gears? Did you hear any changing of speeds?"

She cast her mind back to eight a.m. "I did, actually—there were a couple of gear shiftings and I must say they sounded rather painful."

The inspector rubbed his hands together eagerly. "Now we are getting somewhere. The getaway car is probably one of those ancient, very low horsepower French models still on the road, either a Deux-Chevaux or a Quatrelle. Most likely a Deux-Chevaux."

"What is that?" asked Geoffrey.

"The Citroen Deux-Chevaux is a bit like the old Volkswagen Beetle—it has a very rounded froglike shape," he said, tracing out the car's hump in the air with his hand, "and is kind of like a big tin can with a lawnmower motor in it. Brigitte Bardot drives one in *La Bride sur le Cou*."

Geoffrey laughed. "The ones that are often painted the wildest colors?"

Canal nodded and ordered the hotel owner and the American into Geoffrey's rental car, adding, "We just might be able to catch them, but there is not a moment to lose."

"Let me just run up to my room to get some other clothes first," Geoffrey objected.

"If you venture into the hotel now," Canal tried to dissuade him, "you might end up getting questioned by the police for who knows how long. You will be just fine in the spare clothes you told me you always keep in the trunk," he insisted as he opened the trunk and tossed Geoffrey the garments.

Madame Cochenille made no objection to getting into the car. Not only did she look forward to the opportunity to get the contents of her safe back and avoid having to go through the formalities with the police who most likely would do nothing, but she would get the chance to spend some time with the dashing inspector her hotel guests had now thrice brought into her flight path. The vast majority of men with whom the widow's work at the hotel brought her into contact were married or otherwise attached. Canal, however, seemed to be single, if she could judge by his unadorned ring finger.

XXXV

Mme. Cochenille strapped herself into the front seat and Geoffrey climbed into the backseat of the rental car, as Canal peeled out in pursuit of the safe lifters. The inspector voiced his suspicion that they had headed in the direction of Toulouse, as they were obviously in need of a safecracker and Toulouse was where most criminal activity in the area was centered. The old car the thieves were driving handled very poorly on windy roads, rarely reached its top speed of about forty-five miles per hour, and the distance to Toulouse was considerable—with a little luck, he proffered, they might overtake them.

"The quintessential question, though," he went on, "is who we are following and what they are after."

"What they are after?" Geoffrey reiterated. "The letters, of course."

"How can you be so sure?" Canal asked, glancing toward Geoffrey in the backseat.

"Well, what else could it be?"

"Perhaps Madame Cochenille can help us solve that conundrum," Canal said, looking over at the hotelier in the passenger seat. "What is in the safe?" he asked her. "Is there anything aside from the letters?"

The hotel owner reflected. "Let's see ... A few passports that were given to me by certain hotel guests, and of course some important business papers related to the hotel accounts."

Since she seemed inclined to stop there, the inspector inquired, "Any jewelry?"

"Me, I don't have any jewelry worth keeping in the safe myself," she replied wistfully.

"Did any of your guests ask you to put jewelry in the safe for them?"

The hotelier tried to recall any recent requests, finding it hard to separate in her mind requests guests had made of her three days ago, three weeks ago, and even three years ago. "I believe well," she finally opined, "that the woman in Room 3 gave me a velour bag with jewelry in it a few days ago—she was a bit evasive about just what exactly it was, a necklace of some kind, I think, but I didn't pry. I try to be discreet with my guests."

"Hmm," Canal made a guttural noise. "Do you recall her name or anything about her?"

"I think she called herself Madame Picard. I believe she is one of the people who gave me a passport to hold onto."

"Picard?" cried Geoffrey. "That's the name of the archeological site director! Why would his wife be staying at the hotel instead of with him? Actually, I didn't even think he was married."

"She may not be his wife," Canal cautioned. "There are plenty of Picards in Picardy. Still, it gives one pause ..." Geoffrey's rental car was now barreling along at full tilt, at the inspector's skilled command.

"Maybe Picard heard about the letters and wants them for himself," Geoffrey suggested. Thinking out loud, he added, "He could have instructed his wife to put an inexpensive piece of jewelry in the safe and then stolen the safe himself. That would allow him to get his hands on the letters with impunity and collect the insurance money for his wife's jewelry at the same time."

Canal considered the hypothesis. "He would have reasoned that you would not report the letters missing since you most likely knew full well they were not your legal property. Which would mean no one would be liable to accuse him of having letters that did not belong to him." Perhaps, he speculated to himself, this so-called archeologist had connections with the ring of crooked antique dealers in Bordeaux, who often bought directly from robbers of every ilk, whether gypsies, hired burglars given exact instructions as what to steal in which location, or even everyday thieves.

"Madame Picard does not wear an *alliance*, for whatever that's worth," interjected Mme. Cochenille, the presence or absence of wedding rings being the first thing she noticed about virtually everybody she met.

"Some married people refuse to wear a ring," Canal mused aloud. "It often does not bode well for their marriages, but that is hardly our concern here. Did anyone else give you an item of any kind to put in the safe?"

The hotel owner appeared to think very hard now. "Apart from Hélissenne, let me see … The man in Room 4 gave me something a couple of days ago—I forget what he told me it was."

Geoffrey and the inspector waited for her to go on, as they scoured the landscape speeding by for humpbacked cars.

"Now that I think of it," she eventually continued, "he never did say what it was."

"And since you are so very discreet," Canal added, "you naturally did not ask?"

"Right," she replied, unsure whether she was being flattered or mocked.

"What did this something he gave you look like?" asked Geoffrey.

Mme. Cochenille pictured it in her mind. "It was about the size and shape of a case for reading glasses," she responded, happy to be able to find a description.

"What about its weight?" Canal asked.

"I don't know …"

"Did it feel heavier than a pair of glasses?"

"Much heavier, actually," she replied, recalling her impression. "In fact I remember being surprised at how heavy it was."

Geoffrey and Mme. Cochenille both tried to read Canal's face, which now appeared even more concentrated despite the fact that the driving conditions had improved, the road having become somewhat less narrow and windy.

"Do you think it might be drugs?" the American asked. "Cocaine or heroin?"

"Could be," Canal replied. "But it also could be a weapon, precious metals, or plates to print counterfeit bills with," he added somewhat ominously. "Zen again—"

"Then again what?" asked Geoffrey impatiently.

"It might just be a couple of rolls of ordinary coins."

"Only then there would be no reason to put them in the safe."

"Precisely."

"There probably was at least some metal in the package he gave me," Mme. Cochenille interjected, "because I remember it made a metallic-like noise when it banged against the letterbox when I placed it in the—"

"Letterbox," Canal cried. "What letterbox?"

"The box the letters were in," she replied platitudinously.

Canal turned and peered at Geoffrey in the backseat. "Is this the box you found the letters buried in?"

The American nodded.

Canal struck himself on the forehead with the palm of his right hand and the car swerved slightly on the road. "I cannot believe I never asked you to show me the box! How could I forget a detail like that?"

"What's so important about the box?" Geoffrey asked, perplexed at Canal's display of concern.

"What kind of box was it?" the inspector asked.

"I don't know," Geoffrey shrugged his shoulders and turned toward the hotelier for assistance. "An ordinary metal box."

"Ordinary!" Canal exploded. "There is nothing ordinary about sixteenth or seventeenth century boxes."

It was as if Geoffrey and Mme. Cochenille had been silenced.

"I assume it was key-activated?" the Frenchman asked, craning his neck so he could see Geoffrey in the rearview mirror.

"It was," Geoffrey replied, who was happy to be able to provide at least one piece of information Canal wanted, for he had the impression Canal was glaring at him angrily. "I managed to pick the lock with a hairpin, since we didn't have the key."

"Did you feel around inside?" the inspector asked. Seeing that Geoffrey looked nonplussed, he went on, "Was there a false bottom of any kind?"

"False bottom?" Geoffrey mumbled. "I, I ..."

"*Il faut toujours regarder!*" the Frenchman ejaculated, involuntarily as it were. Calming down, he concluded, "Okay, so you did not think to look. The fact is that boxes from that period often had secret compartments in them," he explained. "There might be something besides letters in the box that we do not know about but that somebody else does."

XXXVI

The road to Toulouse was long and exhaustion now overcame Geoffrey again. While the hotel owner and the inspector talked quietly, as only the French can, in the front seat, he drifted into a semi-sleep state over the next few miles, images of crooked archeologists, insurance assessors, and black market art scalpers dancing in his head.

Mme. Cochenille prattled leisurely, feeling she had an attentive captive audience in the debonair inspector. She swore repeatedly that she would make the vandals who had made off with her safe pay for their actions. But soon she shifted to the increasing difficulties she had running the hotel and restaurant all by herself, the horribly lazy and insubordinate kitchen and housekeeping staff she always had to keep a close eye on, her ever-greater isolation as a widow in a small village in a rather remote location, and the joys of married life. Then, feeling she had been rushing ahead a bit too precipitously, she backtracked to her trouble finding summer help, since all the potential young busboys and housekeeping personnel waited until after the fine summer weather was over to look for work. Could he believe, she asked, that she had been advertising three positions for the past two months and hadn't received a single inquiry? Those imbeciles in the Elysée preferred to pay

France's youth to take a nice long summer vacation instead of giving them incentives to find whatever work they could—just to prevent any potential unrest among them! "What a bunch of—" she exclaimed, but stopped herself before saying anything unseemly in front of the inspector.

Canal shook his head commiseratingly. For, despite her talking a blue streak, he had managed to follow the general thrust of her conversation while keeping his lynx eye on the sometimes treacherous road along the Aude gorge, over the mountains toward the medieval town of Mirepoix, and through the hilly countryside down into the main valley leading to Toulouse. He sympathized with her plight, although not without harboring suspicions that she might well be a trying boss to work for. Her people skills resembled those of many other French people he had known who were off-puttingly gruff on the outside and only nice and even accommodating once you got to know them for a while.

A husband who would give as much of his time to the hotel as she did was, the inspector reflected, clearly one of the few viable business options open to someone in her position, as she would gain the equivalent of three full-time employees without any hiring, contract writing, or worries about being left in the lurch by those who preferred to work the minimum number of months required to collect unemployment checks indefinitely—and, perhaps most importantly, without having to attempt to be diplomatic.

But Canal was neither as taken with the attractive hotelier as she was with him, nor in any way inclined to become an *aubergiste*. He had other cats to whip, as the French put it so infelicitously, other fish to fry—in a word, other preoccupations. Hence he confined his remarks to the generally empathic and kept to himself his speculations as to the effect of continual hundred-hour work weeks on her late husband.

Geoffrey had neither been listening in to their rather one-sided conversation nor admiring the beautiful views. Instead he had been catnapping in the backseat, despite being lurched right and left as Canal guided the car through the narrow defiles and over the sinewy terrain as fast as it could feasibly go without risking anyone's life or limb. Now he was finally alert and scrutinizing every car they passed. He spotted a first Deux-Chevaux off to their left near a farm outside of Pech-Luna, but Canal pointed out that the front of the car was up on cinderblocks as they sped by it.

A second 2CV spotted closer to Saint-Camelle proved, upon inspection, no more roadworthy than the first, and a third one off to the right near Belflou, while eminently navigable, turned out to belong to an elderly couple collecting snails in the long grass beside the road.

As Canal was negotiating a busy roundabout, where the back roads they had been following intersected the main valley roads between Narbonne and Bordeaux, Geoffrey caught a glimpse of a toad-like vehicle in a sizeable parking lot off to their left. The inspector made a split-second change of direction away from his intended route toward Toulouse, and continued back around the traffic circle to take a gander at the car Geoffrey had detected.

It was clearly a 2CV, looked like it was in good condition, and was one of very few cars parked outside a restaurant. "Pearfect," Canal commented with his heavy French accent, "this is just the lucky break I hoped for."

"What do you mean?" asked Geoffrey, leaning toward the front seat to hear better.

"I surmised that, since these thieves have been up and at 'em since no later than seven in the morning, they would get hungry and stop along the way. If I am right," he added, turning out of the traffic circle and into the parking lot of a shop adjacent to the restaurant, "this is precisely what we have been looking for all morning."

XXXVII

The inspector distributed the roles each of them was to play as soon as he parked the car in a discreet corner of the lot and turned off the engine, indicating that he had given some thought while driving to how they would proceed if they managed to catch up with the bandits. Geoffrey donned the long beard and old-timer's beret that Canal had doffed after running into Geoffrey on the trail earlier that morning, since his face might be known to the robbers, and the lad was sent, meerschaum pipe in mouth, to attempt to espy the diners through one of the restaurant windows.

The contrast between the harsh noon sunlight without and the darkness within made it impossible for him to distinguish faces clearly and he was forced to enter the restaurant, furtively glancing into each of the corners of the room so as not to draw attention to himself. Just when he had concluded that he had studied each of the tables to no avail and was about to leave the restaurant, someone exited the men's room right near where he was standing and brushed by him hurriedly, almost knocking him over. It was one of Hélissenne's fellow interns from the dig. If only Geoffrey could remember his name …

He wished it had been Randolph, as he would have liked nothing better than to throttle that excrescence then and there!

Stifling his urge to make this guy pay for Randolph's deeds, Geoffrey noted the number of the intern's companions and then slipped noiselessly out of the restaurant.

Canal listened to Geoffrey's report with interest, but he found less than convincing the student's speculation that this British intern must be in cahoots with Randolph, since Geoffrey himself had once seen the two of them together. The inspector could not fathom why two different teams would have been assembled, unless this second team knew something about the contents of the safe that the first team did not and was engaging in a spot of double-crossing. If Geoffrey were right, on the other hand, he reflected, Hélissenne might well be in far more trouble than he liked to think.

Keeping such cogitations under his proverbial hat, the inspector asked Geoffrey in which part of the restaurant they were seated. The bearded boy calculated that their table was to the left as one entered, leading Canal to conclude that it looked out onto the traffic circle and not onto the parking lot. Geoffrey had no idea how far along they were into their meal, so the Frenchman stationed him near the restaurant's entrance lest they suddenly come out to their car and spoil everything. Should they appear at the restaurant door, the American was to imitate a hoot owl—not the most appropriate animal cry given the time and place, granted, but one of the few he knew how to imitate apart from a monkey and a donkey.

Canal, presumably being unknown to the vandals, had no need for a disguise even if they did just so happen to glance out the auberge window toward their car, but he adorned Madame Cochenille, who *had* met many of the interns face to face at the restaurant, with his now holey but bulky leather jacket and the tan legionnaire's hat he often wore while hiking in the unremitting sun of southern France.

Tucking a newspaper under his arm, he and the hotel owner approached the humpbacked car and divined the shape of the safe under a tropical print beach towel. Overjoyed, they nonetheless confined their expressions of exuberance to the meaningful looks they gave each other and the thumbs-up the inspector displayed in Geoffrey's direction.

Canal was about to wrap a rock near the car in his newspaper and smash the diminutive window pane behind the back door when Mme. Cochenille stopped him with a silent gesture. She pushed in the lower flap of the driver side window which had been—as she suspected, having had one of these cars herself many moons before—left unlocked, it being the kind of window you had to deliberately lock, few people remembering to do so. She then pushed down on the metal lever and opened the door.

The inspector flashed her a broad smile and opened the back window so the hotelier could reach in and dial the safe's combination. He then closed the front door, leaned against the car nonchalantly, and opened up his newspaper to its maximum girth to shroud Mme. Cochenille's torso.

The latter could not stop herself from muttering a couple of nasty swearwords about the difficult angle at which she had to work, but soon had the safe door open. She felt around inside for a bit and extracted a few passports, hotel-related papers, a velvet jewelry bag, a glasses-case-sized package, and finally the letterbox. Then she whispered irritably, "*Les lettres n'y sont plus!*"

"What?" Canal ejaculated.

"The letters are gone," she repeated, just as emphatically.

"That is impossible," he exclaimed as quietly as he could, borrowing an idiotic phrase from Mme. Cochenille's repertoire.

"See for yourself," she said, taking the newspaper from his hands and shielding part of him from view with it.

The inspector glanced in the letterbox and then leaned in the car window, looked in the safe, and felt around in every corner of it. "You do not think they could have already gotten it open, do you?"

"I don't see how. There are something like ten thousand possible combinations."

"I suppose they might have simply gotten lucky."

"Or perhaps they already met up with their safecracker somewhere along the route. In any case, now that somebody else knows the combination, the safe is no longer of any use to me."

"Is it not something of an antique?" Canal asked, looking at it again. "It might actually be worth far more than anything that was inside it—maybe that is what they were after."

"If it is, they were awfully dumb. My late husband picked it up for a mouthful of bread at a flea market in Quillan. It's simply a copy of a Delarue & Grangoir."

"So much the better, because I doubt we could move it anyway. You did not tell Hélissenne the combination, did you?"

"I assure you, I am the only one in all creation who knows it." As if to further emphasize her prudence, Mme. Cochenille added, "I keep the combination in a safe deposit box at the bank just in case I ever forget it."

The Frenchman's mental machinery hummed furiously for a few minutes, as he feigned to read the newspaper alongside his female companion. She remained silent, enjoying his propinquity. He eventually leaned back in the car, and then the hotel owner heard a rustling as of papers, a click indicating that the safe had been closed, and the twirling sound of the dial being spun.

XXXVIII

Bernard Lahron, the British intern from Cambridge University, was pissed! Everything had been going according to plan, at least according to the plan he and his inseparable partner in crime, Allison Foesair, had devised the night before. The coevals had often put his knowledge of historical periods and artifacts and her connections with less than scrupulously honest antique dealers in the British Isles to good use before, but this unexpected boon—landing in their laps owing to a pain-in-the-neck program requirement he had to fulfill for his degree in art history—promised to be their biggest coup ever.

At daybreak that very morning he had been congratulating himself for having played his cards so well since his arrival in France, having ingratiated himself to the girl who, right from the beginning of the internship, seemed to be the luckiest at uncovering valuable medieval artifacts. He had even acted solicitously toward her friend Isabeau, for good measure, running occasional errands for her as though they were tokens of his esteem for the both of them.

Prior to his stay in France, where he had to rely upon charm, wit, and deliberate acts of kindness, his university credentials had always stood him in good stead, establishing his *bona fides* without him having to do anything whatsoever. They had often served as a door-opening calling card, procuring him introductions to the English elite, a clientele that relished and stockpiled every kind of aged object, from medieval gutter stones to Russian icons, from Roman sesterces to Renaissance statuettes. Few of his "discerning" customers seemed to care how they came to acquire these collectibles and fewer still seemed capable of distinguishing them from the admittedly fine fakes turned out by Allison's family-owned business, fakes that Bernard often "returned" to them instead of the genuine article after allegedly having provided them with discreet restoration services, when he didn't simply sell them fakes in the first place.

As a young child, Allison had been told her father and uncles had a workshop in which they restored antiques of all kinds—furniture, canvases, statues, books, documents, you name it—but upon coming of age she had learned that all of this activity was little more than a front. The real bread-and-butter work of the Foesair atelier consisted of turning out multiple copies of borrowed or stolen originals, those copies being sold through an elaborate network of private dealers to wealthy buyers for their own personal viewing pleasure, never to museums where they might be authenticated by independent art experts. If the Foesairs had managed to stay in business for so long, it was due in large part to their prudence.

Ever since Allison and Bernard had overheard Geoffrey and Hélissenne talking excitedly at the café in Lapradelle and on the moonlit trail down the mountain a week before—Bernard translating the little Latin he had understood for Allison who was on holiday, paying him an extended visit—they had been licking their lips in anticipation of the many copies of precious letters they would be able to pass off as the genuine article to a well garnished list of correspondence aficionados known to them. They weren't entirely sure what kind of letters were involved, yet having carefully observed the movements not only of Hélissenne and Geoffrey, but also of Randolph—whom they frequented for lack of anyone more amusing to talk with while in France, enjoying laughing in private at his farfetched self-glorifying stories—they figured they must be worth a small fortune. Which they themselves would know how to turn into a considerably larger fortune!

Secretly despising Randolph, they also despised his primitive methods, preferring the old-fashioned English approach. Fancying themselves a sort of nonviolent, modern-day Bonnie and Clyde, they eschewed the kind of contact with the "client" involved in kidnapping and the like.

In the best French he could muster, which was sorely lacking in nuance and depth of comprehension, Bernard had struck up conversations with somewhat shady-looking characters at bars in the nearby town of Axat and had eventually made a deal with a couple of beefy-looking barflies to help him with a heist *en prêtant main-forte*, as they put it.

All had gone well at the outset: the broad-shouldered blokes had shown up at the chosen place at the appointed time, and had gotten the safe out of the wall and into the car before anyone had sounded the alarm. But the only getaway car they had to offer was the slowest car sold in France in the past half-century, a model named for its famous two-horsepower engine. Worse still, the so-called car, which already was so slow as not to be allowed on the toll highway, promptly blew a flat.

By the time they had figured out how to use the jack, changed the tire, and gotten going again, Bernard was treated to a free French lesson, learning an expression he had never heard before, *panne sèche*. It did not, as he initially thought, have anything to do with dried-out, stale bread of some kind, but rather an empty gas tank. One of the gorillas—the one who had been slapped on the head by the other and called a name Bernard did know, *crétin*—had to walk two miles to the nearest station and back with a can of gasoline, leaving the Brit to champ at the bit by the roadside for an interminable forty-five minutes.

Just as they were finally starting to get within striking distance of their destination, the church bells pealed in a small town along their route off the main highway. The tolling announced not the imminent commencement of the sacraments but the arrival of the noon hour, and the minions' appetites refused to be assuaged without a sit-down lunch.

Bernard tried to appease them by offering to stop at a bakery to buy sandwiches and pastries, but to no avail— they remained obdurate and insisted on a hot meal and drink before they would be willing to go any further. Their friends in Toulouse, they argued, wouldn't want to be disturbed between twelve and three anyway, so what was the rush?

Even if Bernard figured he could handle the 2CV's bizarre stick shift, having measured his skill against many a gearbox in his time, he knew nothing of his recruits' contacts in the city or even where to begin to look for them. He had no choice but to cave.

A restaurant for *routiers* was soon spotted on the left in the little town of Gardouch and they pulled in. The muscle ordered the usual trucker's giant cassoulet special, which included a whole bottle of wine per person, from the surly waitress, and Bernard resigned himself to his fate, though not without plentiful chafing under the collar.

XXXIX

As giant bowls of beans, pork rinds, sausage, and duck were set down before Bernard's workforce, Canal reassembled his troops in Geoffrey's rental car. He opened the proceedings by asking, "Can either of you think of a reason why the letters would not have been left in the safe overnight?"

Geoffrey was shocked and dismayed. "Not in the safe? But they were in there yesterday morning when I got kidnapped," he protested. "After that, of course, I can't say," he added upon further reflection.

"Hélissenne was reading them yesterday in the afternoon," Canal mentioned, updating him. "She had both sets of letters spread out in the dining room." Turning to Madame Cochenille and scrutinizing her face, he asked, "Do you remember when you locked the safe?"

"Oh, things were so crazy last night," she began. "The hotel was completely full and it seems like everyone came down to dinner—I'll never be able to remember."

Canal patted her hand and said softly, "There is no rush at all. Just cast your mind back to last night and try to recall the order in which things occurred."

"Let me see," she began, settling down. "It seems to me that Hélissenne gave me the letters shortly before dinner and I put them in the safe." She gazed out the passenger window while she reflected, so as not to be distracted by schoolgirlish thoughts of Canal. "A little while later I finished preparing some deposits slips and checks I was working on, put them in there too, and locked the door."

"At what time?" the inspector inquired.

"It must have been around seven," she replied automatically, "because after that the first guests began to show up for dinner."

"Did anything related to the safe happen after that?"

"Yes, now that you mention it. Hélissenne came downstairs to ask me how early I usually got up in the morning."

"When was that?"

"I don't know ..." The hotelier did her best to retrieve the information but drew a blank.

"Why did she want to know what time you get up?" Geoffrey eventually asked her.

"Let me see ...," she said, turning toward Geoffrey in the backseat. "Oh my gosh," Mme. Cochenille exclaimed suddenly, "I completely forgot about Hélissenne, what with all the tumult. I hope she got off all right, since I overslept," she concluded. Then, realizing what she had just said, she looked at Geoffrey and amended this, "Well, actually it doesn't matter because you're no longer captive anyway."

Canal, keeping his eye on the interrogatory ball, educed, "So you saw Hélissenne again at some point last night and she asked you to make sure she was up in time. But was that the only thing she wanted to see you about?"

But the hotelier's mind's eye was roving elsewhere. "Now I remember, it was when we were just starting to clean up from the dinner service that Hélissenne came to see me." She looked directly at Canal here. "You had left some time before," she added, without commenting on how attentively she had been

194

watching the well-mannered inspector's comings and goings since his first lunch with Geoffrey at the hotel.

"Apart from wanting you to wake her up," Canal returned to the topic foremost in his mind, "was there not something about the safe that you discussed with her?"

Doing her best to prize her attention away from her present interest in the inspector to the circumstances of the previous evening, Mme. Cochenille admitted, "Yes, there was. She also seemed concerned about having to wake me up in the morning so that I could open the safe and give her the letters."

Geoffrey was struggling to hold on to the thread of the hotelier's mental leapfrog, but Canal was used to hearing stories come out all topsy-turvy.

Seeing Geoffrey's confused face, Mme. Cochenille remarked, "I guess it was kind of contradictory," she seemed to be searching for her words now, "her having to wake me up and wanting me to wake her up."

The fog began to clear slightly for Geoffrey. He opened his mouth to voice a conclusion, "So she—"

"Right," the hotelier interrupted him, "she must have begun by talking about her concern about waking me up to get the letters, and then, when I told her I was an early riser, she asked me to make sure *she* was up by seven at the very latest."

"So she didn't want to bother you with having to open the safe for her in the morning?" Geoffrey asked, finding this a confirmation of Hélissenne's sweet nature.

"Exactly. And even when I said it was no bother at all, she seemed to hesitate, as if she couldn't make up her mind whether to hold onto the letters or leave them in the safe, and kept—"

"Hold onto the letters?" Canal exclaimed. "That would imply she had them in her hands."

"I guess it would," she conceded. "That's right ... Now I remember. Before she asked whether I was an early riser, she asked me if I would be so kind as to open the safe for her again.

I did so right away, and then we talked about what time I got up and what time she needed to be up. And then she seemed to go back and forth about whether to hold onto the letters." Mme. Cochenille looked down suddenly. "I must have had so many other things to do before going to bed that I probably told her to just close and lock the safe once she had made up her mind."

"Marvelous, wonderful!" Canal jubilated and laughed heartily, the sequence of events having finally become clearer. He squeezed Mme. Cochenille's arm affectionately. "That means there is a good chance Hélissenne decided to keep the letters in her room so she would not have to trouble you just a few short hours later. Her consideration for your sleep may well have trumped her concern for the letters' safety."

"What a stroke of luck!" Geoffrey cried.

"*Le hasard fait bien les choses!*" Canal concurred.

Musing to himself, the inspector recalled that the possibility that Hélissenne was possessed of the letters had briefly occurred to him at the hotel that morning when it appeared she had already left in his car. He had let himself be duped into thinking that if the safe had been stolen with such obvious industry, it *must* contain the precious cargo. How could he have allowed his eyes to follow the flamboyant visual effects instead of the prestidigitator's hands? He had taken the bait of semblance.

XL

Trying to reach Hélissenne at the hotel by phone was an exercise in frustration. Mme. Cochenille, who was always at her hotel and who, for obvious reasons, never had much occasion to call herself, didn't remember the first four digits of the ever lengthening French phone numbers, and had to call information. But information no longer worked the way it used to, there now being bizarre new 0800 numbers for each region. She ended up calling her principal bread supplier and, brooking his jeering laughter, asked him for the number of her own hotel. Even then it seemed she was destined to never get an answer, none of the staff seeming to bother to take the helm when the captain was ashore.

While the hotelier painstakingly tried to recall the cell phone number of her head chef, Canal opened the velvet jewelry bag he had extracted from the safe to find a rather shabby looking single-stranded pearl necklace, discovered an odd-looking hunk of stone in the glasses-case, and retrieved nothing but a feather from the secret compartment of the lovely, cedar-lined, Renaissance letterbox. He showed each of them to Geoffrey as they waited outside the phone booth, commenting that the rock was probably the most valuable item of all, appearing to be a rare octahedrite iron meteorite with Thomson structures (or was it Thompson, Canal wondered, having had but a smattering of geology), though still not worth more than a couple of thousand dollars.

After trying a dozen different combinations of numbers, Mme. Cochenille finally managed to reach her chef and he went and got ahold of the assistant hotel manager. Staggering slightly as she came out of the phone booth, Mme. Cochenille informed her two companions that Hélissenne was in jail.

"What could she possibly have done to end up in prison?" asked the dazed American.

As the Frenchwoman indicated that she had no idea whatsoever, Canal found himself reflexively feeling in his holster to ensure that, while having dinner with Hélissenne the night before, he had not accidentally left his gun at the hotel.

XLI

Thoughts of Abelard's overweening and self-destructive ambition swirled around in Hélissenne's head as she lay in bed at Geoffrey's hotel, anxiously anticipating the ringing of the alarm clock, the hike to the Cabane de la Balmette, and the handover. Ruined lives lay scattered about the battlefield of her psyche like so many corpses after the charge of Charlemagne's cavalry.

Had she taken a bit too lightly Geoffrey's ambitious plans to publish the letters they had found in both French and English editions? Perhaps it was a sign that Geoffrey was more interested in making a name for himself than in learning and discovering new things, more interested in making his mark in the world than in his own supposed field of interest. Maybe, when you got right down to it, he was more interested in intellectual prestige than in her …

The thought had never occurred to her before. When she had woken up alone in bed that morning, she had reluctantly entertained the idea that he had merely wished to seduce her and planned to discard her as soon as he had made his conquest. But that he, like Abelard, might be inhabited by a drive bigger than the both of them that could dictate all the wrong choices regarding their future—that was too much!

She reminded herself that she was not sure he really possessed such hubristic ambition—perhaps he had no more than a healthy dose of male drive, the kind she had always admired in her uncle.

She played over in her mind the few discussions they had had about how they would manage to see each other during the coming academic year and the following summer. Doubts that had never before been there crept in one by one, like eels from under a rock. He had spoken as if financial support from his university would be the determining factor in deciding when he could visit her and if he would be able to spend the following summer with her in France. But what if that weren't actually the case?

She suddenly sat bolt upright in the bed. Had she, she asked herself, ever actually asked him how he was paying for his rather extended stay in France? Searching her memory, she seemed to recall him mentioning some kind of travel grant he had received from his department, but she could hardly believe that such funds could cover weeks and weeks in a fine hotel and a rental car to boot! Few if any of her fellow students could afford such extravagant foreign travel for more than a week or two at a time.

Then there were his nice clothes—for he was, she had to admit, a rather tasteful dresser—which must have cost a bundle. And to top it all, he had hired a well-educated, well-mannered, well-spoken private investigator from New York City. That must have set him back more than everything else combined.

Perhaps he had far more money than he let on and was simply hedging his bets by pretending that his ability to come be with her over the next year would depend solely upon his department's beneficence. Maybe he was infinitely more concerned with putting his nose to the grindstone and preparing the letters for publication by a prestigious university press than with taking their relationship further.

The Poitevine leapt out of bed and poured herself a tall glass of water, which she drank as she admired the brilliant moonlight streaming in through the window. Then she closed the shutters and resolved to stop thinking about such absurdities and get if not forty, at least twenty winks.

But agitated thoughts flooded over her again as soon as she laid her head on the pillow. Was ambition, perhaps, a big deal to *her?* Was she in fact more interested in prestige than she admitted to herself, seeking it for herself not directly, but indirectly through Geoffrey?

She did not recall ever having been ashamed or embarrassed that her family lineage could be traced back to the thirteenth century, but she had never—consciously at any rate—played it up or tried to use it to get attention or special treatment of any kind. If she were really some kind of social climber, wouldn't she have been rather more fascinated by Randolph Forster III, who wore his family's British roots on his sleeve like a mafioso his gold chain, than by Geoffrey who, like so many other Americans, could trace his heritage and patronymic no further back than Ellis Island?

This reflection relieved her momentarily, but then she suddenly began to wonder whether she was not perhaps a social climber of a different kind—hadn't she immediately perceived Geoffrey's intellectual qualities and potential, thinking he would go far in the academy? Perhaps she wished to ride *his* coattails to scholarly fame.

Tossing and turning yet again on the queen bed that now seemed too small for her, she wondered whether her choices, like Heloise's, would end up being dictated by aspirations of which she was only dimly aware and which could end up harming both of them …

By three in the morning she had worked herself up into such a lather that she was happy she would be disposing of the letters in a few short hours. *"Bon débarras!* Good riddance!" she thought to herself. "Would that we had never found them in the first place!"

XLII

When she finally awoke and looked at the clock
Geoffrey had brought with him from America,
Hélissenne was bewildered. She had done her best
to set the alarm for six-thirty and had even taken the additional
precaution of asking Madame Cochenille to wake her up by
seven if she had not come down by then.

The clock showed ten-fourteen, which struck her as impossible, her first thought being that the clock must have stopped.
But then she recalled having seen three o'clock come and go
during the night. Feeling around for her watch on the bed-
side table, she brought it into focus in front of her sleep-filled
eyes. Ten-fifteen. She couldn't possibly get to the Cabane de la
Balmette in time!

"That damn American a.m. and p.m. stuff!" she cried,
pulling the sheet back up over her head. She could never
remember which was morning and which was evening. She
directed her fury at herself onto Mme. Cochenille—why hadn't
the innkeeper woken her up as promised?

"Enough!" she reprimanded herself. "Focus on what to do
now." Various options flitted through her mind. The inspector
would be arriving at the Cabane shortly, if he wasn't already
there—perhaps he would be able to take care of things by

himself, she thought hopefully. "But how could he?" were the next words that came to her. "I am the one who has the letters. What will they do to Geoffrey if I don't show up?" She imagined a couple of different scenarios with a mixture of indifference and a feeling of justified vengeance, he being the one who had gotten them into this fix in the first place, encouraging her to excavate the box containing the letters during the night instead of waiting until the next workday when the whole team would have been there to witness the discovery. Then, disgusted at herself, she decided to call Isabeau to ask her advice.

It was ten-twenty-two when Isabeau finally picked up. The latter had been happy to hear the day before from Geoffrey that Hélissenne had been found and was fine. She kidded Hélissenne now about shacking up with her rich American lover and shunning their hovel of a hotel.

"It's not like you think!" Hélissenne protested. "Well, it was a little like you think, but then Geoffrey disappeared, and now I'll never make it to the place where I'm supposed to hand over the letters in exchange for him," she babbled despairingly.

Isabeau was lost. She tried to elicit the story piece by piece from Hélissenne, and get the different components in the right order.

What eventually became clear to Isabeau, as she tried to reconstruct the situation from Hélissenne's rather disjointed and emotional account, was that the Poitevine was ambivalent about rescuing Geoffrey, not seeming to think the effort worthwhile even as she rebuked herself for thinking that way.

"I probably shouldn't tell you, but …" With time inexorably slipping away, Isabeau finally decided to betray Geoffrey's trust. "Whatever your doubts may be about Geoffrey," she told her best friend, "I happen to know that he is planning to spend the coming year in Poitiers with you."

"What?" Hélissenne almost shouted into the phone.

"It was supposed to be a surprise—I think he was going to spring it on you next week," explained Isabeau defensively.

"Who told you that?" Hélissenne asked skeptically, finding it hard to believe her ears.

"Geoffrey himself, of course, you ninny."

"And you didn't tell me?!"

"He *swore* me to secrecy. You wouldn't have wanted me to tell him something about plans *you* meant to surprise *him* with, would you?"

"No, no, of course not. But all the same, so much lost sleep and self-recriminations about phantoms and foolish speculations ..."

The clouds and mists cleared and Hélissenne's decision was swift and unambiguous. "I'm going this instant! I'll call you later." She hastily put down the receiver, grabbed her shoulder bag, and ran out the door.

XLIII

Geoffrey stopped and gazed up at the humble looking, scaffolding-covered entrance to the famed Scentury Club in midtown Manhattan before sauntering in. This would be the first time he had ever set foot in the place as a full-fledged member, rather than as a mere guest, and he savored the moment even though it still remained somewhat unclear to him what the purpose of a private club was.

It must, he felt, be pretty significant, for the inspector, whom Geoffrey had come to think a great deal of over the past two years, swore by it, and had assisted Geoffrey in gaining admittance—which was no easy feat by any stretch of the imagination. One had to be sponsored by two people who had each been a member for at least seven years, and the club had its own sort of initiation ritual, *le cérémonial*, as they called it, as if giving it a French name somehow lent it a more dignified air. Geoffrey had never heard of anything like it before, despite knowing about a great many hazing practices and other initiation rites of passage in force at Yale fraternities.

First, you had to reveal a secret about yourself of which you were none too proud—not to an assembly of all the club's members at least, for discretion was of the utmost importance to the social establishment—but in a book kept in the president's office. This Book, which was always spoken of in reverentially hushed tones, could be consulted by members other than the president no more than once every five years, and only under circumstances deemed to be exceptional by the president himself. And no new member's entries could be read by anyone other than the president before three years had elapsed. So even we shall have to wait before we can know what mortifying story Geoffrey inscribed in the great Book.*

Revealing something rather embarrassing about yourself was at least more or less classic. The kicker was that you also had to reveal a secret about each of your sponsors! These tasty morsels were consigned to the same Book under the direct supervision of the selfsame president, and could be consulted under identical conditions as your own personal secrets. This greatly dampened many members' enthusiasm about having certain friends of theirs who were privy to secrets they wished to remain secret admitted to the club, rendering it still more exclusive. The result was that people with compromising pasts tended to sponsor far fewer new members than those with less skeletons in their closets.

At the outset, Geoffrey had believed that he knew no one at the club other than Canal and that he could disclose no sufficiently juicy secrets even about the Frenchman to qualify as a member. Granted, he did know that Canal looked rather ridiculous in a beret and a long grey beard, but that struck him as pretty slim pickings. And he was aware that a certain Madame Cochenille in the southwest of France had fallen for him in the course of a few short days, but this hardly struck him as the kind of matter that would lead to club admittance.

Spicier perhaps was the admission Canal had made to him on the way to the police station in Quillan when they had

---

*Publisher's note: It is hard to fathom how the narrator could possibly fail to know this.
Narrator's note: The publisher should mind his own beeswax, instead of trying to tell the narrator what he should and should not know.

208

gone to get Hélissenne released from custody: that after the hotel owner had taken the passports of her paying guests out of the safe in the back of the Deux-Chevaux, he had slipped into the safe some worthless letters written in Latin on parchment—but, more importantly, a couple of fake passports he occasionally used when he traveled and wished to remain incognito—to make the purloiner believe that the safe had not been tampered with. Not only did Canal carry a gun, despite having long since retired from the French secret services. He also traveled under different names, faces, and nationalities! This particular tidbit had tickled the club president's fancy and thus proven sufficient.

It had been easier, as it turned out, with the second sponsor whom Geoffrey recognized in the reading room one day as he and Canal were walking by it on the way to the dining room for yet another copious repast. It was Cardrich O'Neil, a professor of French literature whom Geoffrey had known in his undergraduate days and who had since become dean of a prestigious college. O'Neil's marriage had been of the long-distance commuting variety back in Geoffrey's undergraduate days, and Geoffrey, who had done some odd jobs for him during the summers, had occasionally noted a good deal of entertaining of attractive coeds going on in O'Neil's home while the cat was away, so to speak.

The professor, who had always liked Geoffrey as both a student and a handyman, also liked his libations and other stimulants potent and frequent, and appeared to have long since forgotten all about the compromising scenes Geoffrey had witnessed. No allusion to them was ever made in the course of the several conversations Geoffrey had with him prior to requesting that he sponsor his admission to the club. O'Neil made no objections to serving as an official *parrain*, as he called it, assuming perhaps that Geoffrey would simply reveal that one day in class he had slipped and said Felman instead of Mehlman or dickless instead of ridiculous—Geoffrey had always remembered that last one, he and his puerile classmates getting a lot of mileage at the time out of dicta like "you can't take the dickless out of ridiculous" and "you can't take the master out of masturbation."

As he climbed the steps to the club's main entrance, was greeted by the doorman, and navigated the various passageways to the sunroom, Geoffrey regarded the few members present at that early hour with an admixture of curiosity and suspicion. At thirty-two, he was far and away the club's youngest member, and yet he still often felt like and even thought of himself as a mere adolescent. His analysis with Jack Lovett, a practitioner recommended to him by Inspector Canal (for Canal, unbeknownst to Geoffrey, still didn't entirely trust Lovett with attractive women like Erica Simmons and Hélissenne and had sent him the male rather than the female portion of the formerly Latin-speaking couple), had shown that to him in spades, even just in the last session from which he had emerged not ten minutes before. "Juvenile" was the last word to have passed Geoffrey's lips, the analyst himself never using such terms, before the session came to a rather abrupt end.

Selecting from the display racks a stuffy-looking financial newspaper published in England—you couldn't get any more adult than that, after all, he thought—Geoffrey seated himself in an unbelievably comfortable armchair and tried to focus on the front-page stories. Economic downturns and tensions with the Chinese held his attention only with great difficulty. His mind soon drifted back to the topic of being mature or, rather, immature, as his parents had often claimed he was.

"What does it really mean to be immature or adolescent?" he wondered, knowing full well that these were everyday words people used to stigmatize forms of behavior they just didn't happen to like. *Adolescence*, he recalled, came from the Latin "to grow" and an adolescent used to simply mean someone big enough to have children. It applied to people from fourteen to twenty-eight—scholars ignorant of this fact had, he smiled at the recollection, drawn the silly conclusion that Heloise was but an innocent girl of sixteen who was exploited by a dirty old Abelard twice her age when their relationship started, instead of an accomplished young woman in her twenties. The word sometimes even applied to folks as old as thirty-five, thus including Geoffrey himself. He was painfully aware that what his contemporaries referred to as adolescence—being dependent on one's parents, not yet ready to run a household of one's own, and not taking responsibility for one's own life and actions—had been getting longer and longer for the past couple of centuries, it taking youths like himself far more years to complete their education and training and forge out into the world on their own than even a Johnny Tremain from the seventeen hundreds who was an apprentice at age sixteen. There wasn't much he could do about his seemingly interminable education, he thought, mentally letting himself off the hook for that facet of modern-day adolescence. Or was there?

He had long since finished all his Ph.D. coursework, but his dissertation was far from complete. Indeed, he had not yet really even settled on a thesis topic. He *had* begun to publish—finally, he felt, for it was after all the sine qua non in academia—but still felt like he knew almost nothing and could say little of import in his own name. Throwing himself wholeheartedly into the cooperative project with Hélissenne had been possible precisely because it had fallen into his lap and didn't require him to take a stand of any kind.

But his dissertation—*that*, he felt, was a horse of a different color. He realized now that he took the choice of topic way too seriously, thinking of his thesis as some kind of magnum opus sketching out the direction of his whole life's work, rather than as just a way station along the circuitous path of his burgeoning intellectual development. It had to be so momentous that none of the ideas for it that he came up with on his own nor any of the topics that his professors proposed seemed to him to

211

fill the bill, being too specialized, sounding overly technical, or targeting an excessively narrow audience.

Sitting there with the newspaper hanging limply in his hand, Geoffrey reflected that he had misled, if not outright lied to the inspector when he had told him in the mountains two years earlier that while he might not have that good an idea what he wanted to do with Hélissenne, he at least had a pretty good idea of what he wanted to do academically. The fact was that he was paralyzed by his own ambition to make his mark on the world, to astound and make quaver everyone in his field and in related fields—the more fields the better. The walls of Jericho would have to tremble and fall! In a word, he was rendered immobilized by his own striving for greatness.

It was not as if his parents had been unsupportive. In their concern not to determine his future path in life for him, they had applauded nothing he did especially loudly, all of his achievements being greeted with the same mild praise. Their liberal-minded attempt to allow him to find and develop his own interests ultimately backfired, from his vantage point, their son desperately seeking instead some grand deed or accomplishment that would finally win their unadulterated, enthusiastic approval.

He had racked his brains trying to figure out what geste, what feat could possibly have the effect he desired upon them, and had been doing the same thing his whole life since with other people he looked up to or saw as authority figures. The indistinct idea occurred to him that perhaps "maturity" had something to do with not trying to shoot the moon in everything he did, with accepting his own limitations ... Could that be what Freud meant by that most reviled, indecorous term of his, castration?

His desperate striving to impress was but the tip of the ambition iceberg, Geoffrey now realized, and after one short

212

year of analytic work it had begun to sink in that even this one tip would take some considerable time to topple, so massively underpinned was it.

A few of his friends with less liberal kinfolk accused their parents of dictating their pathway in life to them. Yet their predicament seemed enviable to him: they knew what they were supposed to do in life to please people, their parents first and foremost, and it was usually something they were quite capable of accomplishing. At least Geoffrey thought so. His problem was quite the opposite—his parents just wanted him to be happy doing whatever he wanted to do. What a crushing load it had been upon his shoulders to figure out what it could possibly be that *he* wanted to do ...

So heavily did these thoughts weigh upon Geoffrey that he almost slid off his armchair when someone tapped him gently on the back, exclaiming, "Geoffrey, my boy. Fancy meeting you here!"

Although Geoffrey had come to the club after his session that day with no expectation of running into Inspector Canal, he had harbored a secret hope that the latter's jovial face would be there to greet him, since he felt somewhat lost both at the club and in New York City in general, being more comfortable in his New Haven college town environment or out striding through the mountains of New England.

Canal was looking as fresh and chipper as ever, having just returned from a series of invigorating hikes in the Queyras area of the Alps among the *mélèzes*, unusual larch-type trees that turn aspen yellow in the fall and shed their evergreen-like needles in the winter. The Frenchman had not yet lost his summer color to Manhattan's autumn climes, and seemed to be thoroughly absorbed in a new case he was working on, about which he gave Geoffrey but a few sketchy details, involving the murder of a psychoanalyst-in-training by a patient at a lower Manhattan psychoanalytic institute.

213

"Sounds pretty scary to me," Geoffrey commented, picturing himself, with a slight shudder, eviscerating his own analyst with a long hunting knife.

"Scary? Merely to be expected, I would say, given how analysts are selected and trained in our times."

"You've never told me how you come to know so much about psychoanalysis."

"Have I not?" Canal asked disingenuously. "It is a long story ..." Rising suddenly from the armchair next to Geoffrey's in which he had seated himself on first arriving in the sunroom, the Frenchman declared, "I am famished! What do you say you treat me to that lunch you have owed me these past two years?"

Geoffrey had forgotten all about this singular debt to the inspector, but it all came back to him now. At the end of their adventures in southwestern France, Geoffrey had discreetly drawn Canal aside and gingerly broached the topic of the astronomical fee the American must inevitably owe the Frenchman for his assistance, a highly approximate reckoning of which the student had made the night before, including the number of days Canal had spent with him and Hélissenne, the hotel and restaurant bills, the cost of replacing forged documents, and, last but not least, a new leather jacket to replace the one he had cut to shreds to sheathe Geoffrey's lacerated feet. But after joking that Geoffrey should fill out a check for fifty thousand francs, Canal had dismissed the whole question of emolument, making the single peculiar demand that Geoffrey buy him lunch at the time and place of the inspector's own choosing. So here it was, the moment had finally arrived.

Geoffrey immediately acceded to Canal's request, and as they were being seated at a cozy corner table in a nearby Perigordian restaurant, Geoffrey raised a question that had preoccupied him for some time after their work together in France. "Why do you help people out with their problems and headaches? What interest can you possibly find in such things?"

Canal eyed the boy keenly, as if to read in his face the motives behind the question. Detecting nothing more than genuine perplexity there, Canal glanced cursorily at the menu he knew virtually by heart and replied, "I enjoy delving into people's psyches and into the mysteries they stumble upon in life, whether personal or historical."

"Historical mysteries?" Geoffrey queried, opening the utterly unfamiliar menu that had been deftly placed before him by a liveried waiter. "Were there any in my and Hélissenne's case?"

Canal was flabbergasted. He signaled the waiter and, soliciting Geoffrey's permission to choose for him with a minute hand gesture, ordered *magret fumé* and a sumptuous *cassoulet à la façon de Castelnaudary* in addition to an old Minervois wine from the vineyards near Carcassonne and the usual trimmings, before replying to Geoffrey's query. "Apart from the question of whether your love would endure," he stated, winking at the young man, "there was the initial uncertainty around the authenticity of the two sets of letters."

Geoffrey nodded.

"And then there was the tripartite question of the letters' movements: first, from Abelard's personal collection to the monastery at Clairvaux where Jean de la Véprie copied them in the late 1400s; second, from Clairvaux into the possession of Marguerite de Navarre, in southwest France, where she made a complete copy of them; third, from Mont-de-Marsan, her so-called hermitage or writing retreat, to a Cathar fortress reutilized in the seventeenth century as an outpost on the Franco-Spanish border. Are there not enough mysteries there to satisfy anyone's appetite?" he exclaimed.

"I guess I never gave any thought to the letters' trajectory, thinking only of their literary significance."

"Of which they have plenty. But there is far more than just that. I suspect that there is an intimate relationship between the intriguing and oft contradictory claims made in them about love," the inspector postulated, "and their passing from hand to hand over the course of the centuries."

"How so?"

"It is well known, for example, that Jean de Meun—a poet who, like all poets, was interested in love, having written *The Romance of the Rose*—managed to get his hands on a copy of Heloise and Abelard's later letters. And it is clear that Petrarch, the infamous author of *The Satyricon*, who was no less interested in the topic of love, read them and even made now approving, now misogynist comments in the margins of his copy. He might even be said to have fallen in love with Heloise on the basis of those letters!

"In other words," the Frenchman continued, "the people most interested in love—and is it not always for at least partly if not primarily personal reasons?—were the ones who wanted to get ahold of these letters, which is why it is no surprise that Marguerite de Navarre had them for at least some short time. She must have thought they contained a great many important notions about love since she took the trouble to copy them, no small feat in the sixteenth century, given how difficult the text on parchment must have already been to read at that time." The inspector looked approvingly at the smoked breast of duck that the waiter had just silently set down before them and lifted a first morsel to his lips. "Most delectable," he exclaimed, and clinked glasses with Geoffrey, finding that this particular luncheon cum honorarium was getting off to a fine start.

"The trajectory of these letters," Canal concluded, "is thus likely to have been based on the interests of prominent poets and writers from the twelfth to the seventeenth centuries, who perhaps even hid them at Puilaurens to prevent them from being seized by Louis the Fourteenth's censorship squad."

216

"And you think you will be able to trace all of the letters' movements over such a long period of time?" the classicist inquired after he had swallowed the entirety of the delicious smoked appetizer.

"I highly doubt that, although the box the letters were in may yet hold clues to how they ended up at Puilaurens."

"Then of what interest could their trajectory be to you?" asked Geoffrey, sipping his wine contemplatively.

"A question can be of great interest even if one suspects that it involves imponderables, even if one will never know the full answer to it or know the answer beyond the shadow of a doubt," Canal replied, looking at the boy intently. "We must always attend to the question of *scibilitas*, knowability, and respect the limits of knowledge—whether something cannot be known simply for the time being or cannot be known for structural reasons. But that does not stop us from learning all kinds of interesting things within those bounds or from advancing hypotheses which, like most hypotheses when you come right down to it, cannot be either confirmed or refuted."

As Geoffrey continued to look puzzled by Canal's interest in questions that might well be impossible to answer—the kind of questions he had been taught to carefully avoid in his scholarly work as a budding academic and which he knew to be considered worse than poetry by many of the philosophers of science he had studied—Canal added, "Let me give you an example. You recall that the professor friend of yours who gave you my name and number has a friend here in New York whom I assisted regarding a counterfeit form of the Chartreuse liqueur."

Geoffrey recalled the story and indicated that he did so with his fork, momentarily removing it from its more usual service sampling the cassoulet the waiter had recently placed before him.

"In the course of that investigation, I learned that the original formula for that elixir was written in Occitan, which flew in the face of the accepted perspective that botanical knowledge was, at that time, confined to and conveyed exclusively within Latin culture."

Geoffrey gave his fork a slight rolling motion to indicate that he was listening and wished the inspector to go on, even if his eyes were glued to the steaming specialty of Castelnaudary.

"After I left you and Hélissenne in Gincla two summers back," Canal accordingly continued, "I stopped off at a number of libraries and museums, and although I was unable to discover the author of the formula, the more I learned, the more likely it seemed to me that at least some of the botanical knowledge required to concoct such a formula had arrived in Catalonia via the Moors and possibly even the Visigoths." Canal smiled broadly at this, hoping, as he tasted another forkful of the second course, to have made the significance of this find and thus of his overarching point clear to even the dullest of wits.

But the history of Europe after the fall of the Roman Empire was, to Geoffrey's unhistorically trained mind, dotted by few landmarks beyond Marie Antoinette, the French Revolution, Napoleon, and World Wars I and II. He looked at the Frenchman uncomprehendingly, and eventually just shrugged his shoulders.

The inspector shifted in his chair, moving a couple of inches back from the table, and tried a different tact. "When you endeavor, for example, to understand something you did or decided upon in your past, you sometimes get to the point in your psychoanalytic work where no ultimate explanation seems to be forthcoming or absolutely sure."

At this, Geoffrey's brow involuntarily transmuted into the likeness of a painter's seagull.

"Try as you might," Canal went on, having chewed thoughtfully for some moments, "there seems to be nothing new you can remember about that time, nothing that you have not already explored and re-explored, having gone over the same ground again and again, and all you can do is hypothesize about why you did what you did or made the decision that you made. Freud called that a construction, as opposed to a recollection, making it clear that we sometimes have to content ourselves with constructions and reconstructions of the major turning points or tipping points in our lives, there being something *insondable*—I forget how you say that in English," he said, appealing to Geoffrey for assistance.

"Unfathomable?" Geoffrey suggested, having worked hard on his French while in Poitiers the previous year, and happy to be able to contribute something to the conversation other than plenteous sounds of mastication.

"Right. There being something unfathomable about it or it having taken place so early in our lives that our memories of it, such as they were, cannot be accessed in the present, lacking the inscription in language, time, and our individual history so characteristic of the memories that *are* accessible to us." He wiped the corners of his mouth with his napkin.

Perceiving Geoffrey's closed features, Canal added, "I am forgetting, of course, that you have only been at it for about a year so far, so you probably have not had the kind of experience I am talking about yet."

Geoffrey lifted his glass to his mouth and took a meditative sip.

"In any case," the inspector commented, "it is the continual deepening and broadening of learning that is enlivening, the continual revision and reconstruction of our ideas that is stimulating, not attempting to demonstrate mastery, not the scholarly fixing on paper or setting in stone of certainties. Certainty is vastly overrated—I mean, when it comes to knowledge, naturally, not desire. For in the latter case, decided desire beats the hell out of uncertain, undecided desire every time!"

The American, finally tasting the liquid he had sipped, had to make a special effort not to spit it out, having mistaken his

219

water glass for his wine glass. "What exactly are you saying?" Geoffrey finally protested. "That we don't actually know anything, other than what we want?"

"I am saying," Canal noted with satisfaction that the American seemed to have perked up a little bit, "that it is at the very moment that you believe you have mastered something or achieved certainty in a specific field that you have become its dupe, that you are the most thoroughly deluded."

Geoffrey's face suggested that this statement had hit home, the creases in his forehead smoothing out. "You mean like it's at the very moment when I am most thoroughly convinced that things between Hélissenne and me will work out that I do something to make them go terribly wrong," he asked in a half-assertive, half-questioning tone of voice.

The waiter set down their walnut-based dessert before them, along with a half-bottle of Muscat de Frontignan in its famous twisted bottle, pouring small amounts into tiny glasses for each of them and making himself scarce. "Now zere is a fascinating illustration that would never have occurred to me," Canal exclaimed, as he lifted his glass and proposed a toast, "To remaining non-dupes of supposed certainties."

"To *becoming* non-dupes of our own bright ideas," Geoffrey amended the toast. The two, smiling impishly, clinked glasses.

After Geoffrey had expressed his surprised approval of the dessert wine and Canal had refilled their glasses to the brim, the Frenchman upped the ante with a further toast, "May we be dupes only of the unconscious, following it everywhere, lest we be led astray by our conscious understandings."

XLIV

The lunch hour had come and gone, the courses had all been done justice and the wines given appropriate homage. Saying his adieus to Canal, Geoffrey directed his steps to the train station and returned to New Haven.

Canal, for his part, consulted his watch and decided to make a little visit that he had been meaning to make for some time, despite the cloudy, blustery, and somewhat threatening weather. Exiting the restaurant, he flagged down a taxi and climbed out only after reaching the Cloisters on the Upper West Side.

Meandering around the astonishingly pink marble courtyard, the other half of which he had visited many a time and oft at its original location at Saint-Michel de Cuxa in the Pyrenees, he paused to admire an elaborately sculpted capital atop a finely tapered column. He was surprised to discover someone, who at first had been partly hidden from his view, regarding the same capital from the other side of the pillar. Shifting his gaze from the upper reaches of the column to his fellow admirer and refocusing his eyes, he was astonished to realize that it was Geoffrey's wife, Hélissenne.

Startled out of her solitary meditations, Hélissenne greeted the inspector warmly and effusively. Although they had seen each other several times over the past two years, it had always been in the company of Geoffrey, and three-way conversations are never quite the same as two-way. After Hélissenne's initial shock at running into someone she knew in the vast metropolis that is New York City, the Frenchman remarking that it was perhaps not as strange as all that given their shared interest in Romanesque art and architecture—not to mention the fact that this was undoubtedly the most significant example thereof on the North American continent—they agreed to visit this portion of the edifice as well as the remainder of the museum together.

Strolling along the two sides of the cloister courtyard that had been sold by unscrupulous merchants to local French bathhouse developers and then to American art exporters who had ultimately saved the structure from destruction, they examined the different representations of sin, people being swallowed by monsters by way of punishment, miracles, and explicit nudity.

As they regarded the touching marital scenes depicted in the delicately carved Ivory of Marriage once back indoors, Hélissenne commented on the importance in love of the endless gestures expressing love for another that must be engaged in every day.

"Which leads to a sort of infinite ethics of love," Canal observed, "not to the poet's view that love is a pebble laughing in the sun." Musing for a moment, he added, "Or perhaps, rather, an ethics of infinite love."

This last formulation made Hélissenne stop dead in her tracks.

"What is it?" Canal asked, concerned, seeing tears begin to form in the lovely girl's eyes.

"It's that infinite part," she replied brokenly. "I love Geoffrey with a love that can scarcely be called infinite. I do love his sense of humor, his strength, and his can-do attitude, but I also find much in him that is hard to love. But as imperfect as my love for him is, it is already far too strong for his taste."

Her tears began to flow freely and Canal put a fatherly arm around her shoulders and drew her toward his side.

"You'd think he wanted me to stop loving him altogether so he could be the only one of us who loves," she sobbed quite unreservedly now. Turning to look at the inspector, despite her shame at the waterworks, she added, "Can't both people in a couple love, or does it have to be one-sided? Can't love be mutual?"

"It can be, but I am sorry to say it is rather rare. You have stumbled upon one of the major obstacles to love, this one related to the male of the species."

He took the disconsolate Poitevine by the elbow and she allowed her steps to be guided toward a quiet part of a nearby medieval garden where they could talk more privately at their leisure, few visitors venturing beyond the covered paths owing to the inclement weather. They sat on the edge of an ancient well that once stood worlds away from there in time and space.

Knowing of the friendship between Canal and Geoffrey, Hélissenne was initially loath to complain about him to the inspector, but he encouraged her to unburden herself. Her sense, she told him, was that Geoffrey seemed to run away from or negate her loving gestures, apparently wanting to be the only one in the couple who loved, who was working at their relationship. She almost got the feeling that he wanted to feel that his love for her was unrequited, that he was the only one compromising and making sacrifices for both of their sakes, not her. "Does he have some sort of martyr complex, in your estimation, wanting me to be the *domina*, the cruel Lady to whom he is duty bound?" she asked. "Or does he have to be forever pursuing someone who is impossible to capture?"

"It strikes me as a bit more complicated than that."

223

"I try to put myself in his shoes to figure out why he could possibly want *not* to be loved, but I can't for the life of me fathom it."

"We can never mentally or imaginatively put ourselves in anyone else's shoes with a high degree of accuracy. Our whole life experience has been different from the other person's and all we can imagine is what it would be like to put *ourselves*—as we already are, with all our own thoughts, feelings, and troubles—into someone else's specific love relationship or work predicament. The project of empathy fails here: without having experienced everything the other person has experienced, we can never even begin to imagine what it is like to *be* them or fathom why they do what *they* do and want what *they* want unless we look at things more structurally."

"How do you mean?"

"I mean we might have a fighting chance of grasping what is driving Geoffrey if we consider the whole of his life and not just the present moment. My guess, and of course it is no more than that since Geoffrey and I are hardly intimate friends, is that what we are dealing with here is repetition. And it is not the benign Kierkegaardian type where, when things come around again, you do not just get everything you lost back again, but you get twice as much as before, like Job—no, this is straight, unadulterated, life-rending repetition."

Hélissenne's eyes narrowed. "Repetition of what?"

Seeing her surprise, Canal replied, "Nothing terribly remarkable, I suspect. Just the usual Oedipal stuff." The clouds did not part letting the sun shine through for Hélissenne, so he continued, "Everyone focuses on the male child's anger and death wishes directed at his father for breaking up the boy's cozy twosome with his mother. But a boy often becomes fixated on the denouement of his relationship with his mother: he feels his love for her was always true and unlimited, whereas her love proved to be false, limited, and indeed for someone else. He is hurt, believing as he does that

224

he was betrayed, jilted by her, neglected in favor of a rival, and this he repeats."

"Why on earth would he repeat it if it hurt him? I thought people repeated pleasurable experiences."

"There you touch on the very nature of *la bête humaine*. We human beings are strange animals, indeed, for we keep repeating what we never manage to accomplish or fix, and we become attached to our misery. We even learn to love it more than ourselves, more than our own possible happiness."

"I'm sure *I* would never do anything like that!"

"Maybe not, but I would not count on it," Canal retorted, a trifle surprised at such a comment from one undergoing psychoanalysis, but reminding himself that she was a mere novice after one short year in the mines. "Faced with such suffering, most of us find some way of redeeming it in our own eyes—Geoffrey, perhaps, thought of himself as heroic for remaining true to his mother despite her perfidy and betrayal. Maybe he came to think of himself as morally superior to her, and by extension to other women, overflowing with a kind of righteous indignation at their unreliability or fickleness."

Hélissenne found herself nodding as Canal speculated about her husband, but the Frenchman, whose eyes had come to rest on the entablature above some nearby columns, did not immediately notice. "There are, of course," he added as a caveat, "many variants of the Oedipal drama—some men *can* stand to be loved but *cannot* stand to be asked for anything by a woman, feeling that they were monumentally swindled when their mothers showed they preferred their fathers and believing that all women have an infinite debt to pay off to them for that. Still others—"

"Geoffrey fits better the first example you gave," interjected Hélissenne, as the inspector seemed to be moving away from the nub. "He always seems to be trying to find a reason to believe that I prefer some other man to him. It's utterly preposterous, but if I make the slightest positive comment about

225

an actor in a film or a hero in a novel, he latches onto it and won't let go. At first he seems triumphant and then he gets despondent about it. He's convinced there must be some other man whom I am secretly pining for, whether my old boyfriend François or even my uncle Filbert. It's the silliest thing I've ever heard!"

"And yet it *has* to be true for him, his love has to be unrequited—it is a sort of subjective necessity for him," the inspector asserted. "In certain cases, a man is blind to the love his partner has for him, because the present is cast by him in the die of the past, repetition requiring that a woman have no genuine love for him. And in other cases, his compulsion to reproduce the past goes so far that he succeeds in driving his partner into some other man's arms, thereby confirming his preconceived notion that she did not truly love him in the first place. He pushes her away by constantly accusing her of infidelity and by insistently playing the role of the magnanimous, self-sacrificing lover."

"But women too need to love! How's a girl to love in such circumstances?"

"Even someone as insightful as Freud believed—based, no doubt, on his own love predicament—that women, like cats, want to be loved but have no need or desire to love, at least none that cannot be satisfied through caring for children."

Hélissenne's face evinced perplexity at this. "I do love children, and hope to have a few of my own some day. But loving a spouse is not at all the same as caring for children!"

"No kidding. One is always tempted to translate *one's own* feelings about the opposite sex into some sort of fixed characteristic. Freud felt his love for his wife was not adequately returned by her and concluded that women never love anyone but themselves—save their children, who he understood to be mere narcissistic extensions of themselves in any case. To his way of thinking, women simply want to be loved, period, the end." He gave Hélissenne a meaningful look here and added,

"More likely, though, he wanted to be able to think of himself as the one who loved faithfully, and took an odd satisfaction in feeling lovelorn and gypped by his wife."

"How can you deal with someone who refuses to be loved?" she asked, jumping up from the ancient stone well that had been serving them as a bench and pacing for a moment.

Canal waited, unsure whether the question was rhetorical or not.

"I suppose," Hélissenne began, haltingly, to answer her own query, "a woman could express her love by playing along, by *letting* her man act superior, act like he is the only one in the relationship to love. But it sounds awfully unfulfilling to me."

"The very fact that you thought of it is yet another proof of your love for Geoffrey. But I agree with you that it would be consummately unsatisfying in the long run. Perhaps his analysis will loosen things up there."

"I certainly hope so," Hélissenne cried, sitting back down, "but when? Why is it taking so long?"

Her interlocutor looked at her compassionately, cognizant of the difficulty of her situation while also recognizing the myriad twists and turns of the analytic process. "Time is a funny thing," he replied, an analogy having occurred to him. "It took you only two minutes to get yourself dragged from the hotel in Gincla to the police station in Quillan two years ago: you asked a gendarme in the lobby to move his vehicle because it was blocking the car you had parked somewhere behind the restaurant instead of in the hotel lot, your eyes involuntarily darted toward the safe when he mentioned that there had been a robbery, and you said something about an agreed-upon meeting place for an exchange, and with no further ado he concluded you must have aided and abetted the crime. What it took you two minutes to get into, it took us two hours to get you out of!"

Recollecting the absurdity of the misunderstanding that had occurred with the dunderheaded police officer at the hotel that morning and the endless, tiresome formalities that had ensued—which had at first rankled but later become a subject of much mirth between herself and Geoffrey—Hélissenne's face brightened slightly and she nodded.

"As for Geoffrey, it took him over three decades to get into the mess he is in," Canal remarked, "so I suspect it is going to take some time for him to work his way out of it. Conscious vigilance is incapable of putting a stop to repetition, the latter always finding a way around the former. Working through is required and no twelve-session therapy can provide that. Geoffrey will probably need a few years to begin to change in any really noticeable way."

"You mean I should prepare myself for a few years of continued frustration?" she inquired, looking at him imploringly.

"I am afraid so," he replied, putting his arm around her shoulders anew and giving her a little hug.

By way of thanks for his willingness to talk about all this with her and for his comforting gestures, she kissed him on the cheek. "I'm no saint either, I'm sure," she eventually proffered, "but what I don't get is that Geoffrey wasn't at all like this at first, at least it seemed to me—it's really only been in the last six months or so."

"These kinds of repetitions do not always set in right away. I once knew a couple for whom everything seemed to go fine until a couple of years into their marriage when the female portion of the couple became progressively convinced that her husband did not love her and that he must be in love with some other woman—an older woman he worked with at his office."

Hélissenne was listening intently, so Canal went on, "She had felt particularly jilted by her own father when, after the death of her mother, he remarried and had a child with his second wife, a woman with whom his daughter had typically horrible stepmother-stepdaughter relations. As painful as it was to her to feel she was being dumped by her father for this other woman, she appeared to be unable to stop herself from eventually reproducing the same scenario with her own husband."

"What was in it for her?"

"My sense was that she enjoyed—without knowing it and certainly without ever owning it—seeing herself as the victim of a man's callousness. This was, after all, precisely how her mother had always portrayed her relations with her husband to her daughter. I guess there was some sense of moral superiority and righteous indignation that she, like her mother, was able to derive from the scenario."

"What ever happened to them?" asked Hélissenne, as if concerned that their fate would somehow mysteriously determine her own.

"She almost pushed him so far as to make overtures to the older woman at work, whom he had never given a moment's notice before, but fortunately his wife's analysis reached a first critical juncture and she was able to temper her recriminations in time to forestall that."

"I sure hope we never get to that point. It seems like such useless drama."

"Yes, the Oedipal drama tirelessly returns, serving as the daily neurotic bread of people's lives. It takes considerable analytic work to put a stop to the repetition."

"Does no one escape it without analysis?"

"Do you know anyone who does not seem to be repeating something beyond her control?"

Her best friend briefly flashed through her mind, but Isabeau's attraction to men her closest friends were involved with struck her as quite neurotic, even if she did not know what Isabeau might be repeating thereby. Next she thought of François, but his way of attaching himself to girls all the more thoroughly when they made it plain they were not terribly interested in him clearly disqualified him too.

She looked up at Canal and shook her head.

229

It was only later, while she was riding the train back to Connecticut, that she asked herself what *she* might be repeating. Her abundant self-doubts struck her as a sure sign of malady that she would be thrilled to see evaporate for good. She found herself wondering next whether Canal himself might not have the teensiest neurotic bone in his body and, if so, what the inspector himself might be repeating ...

XLV

I had just finished perusing some recently published correspondence—the last line of which was "Nothing could ever stop me from loving you with a love without measure"—when Canal came into the reading room at the Scentury Club. I had met the inspector some years before when he and I collided, both reaching for the same rare volume on the uppermost shelf of a bookcase in that very same library. We had quickly discovered that we had overlapping interests and had since enjoyed a great many discussions over a glass of fine port or sherry, when it wasn't over a five-course dinner in the club dining room. I knew him to be a well-read Frenchman, albeit with unusually wide tastes—far too wide, perhaps, for my own liking, I admittedly having been a somewhat stodgy scholar of a narrow literary genre before becoming a shrink.

The inspector noticed me reading in a corner by the window and recognized the cover of the book I was holding in my hands in the instantaneousness of a glance.

"*Ah, mon cher Edgar,*" he began warmly—such a French preamble always being, in my experience, a sign of enthusiasm and affection on his part—"I see that you are reading one of the trufflesque fruits of my labors in the southwest of France."

I had been ready for many comments on the volume from such an avid and eccentric reader, but certainly not this one, which surprised me exceedingly.

Remarking my astonishment, Canal proffered, "Is it possible that I neglected to tell you about my role in securing these letters? I must be getting forgetful indeed!"

"I knew that you had met the editor whom you referred to me some time ago, and have naturally heard some of her reflections on conversations you had with her back then as her analysis has proceeded," I added, almost whispering so as to disclose to no one other than himself that the young Frenchwoman had, in effect, been following through on her therapy with me, even though we were the only ones in the spacious room and I was quite sure he already knew this. "But I had no idea you yourself assisted in, as you put it, *securing* the letters."

I invited him to be seated in the buttery-soft leather armchair next to mine and offered him a libation, which he accepted with bonhomie as he told me a tale that struck me as almost implausibly incredible.

A number of things puzzled me in the yarn he wove. Being privy, as I was, to a great deal of information about Hélissenne's life and relationship with Geoffrey, I knew that Geoffrey had spent a year in France with Hélissenne, that they had married soon thereafter, and that she had then moved to the States with him while he tackled his dissertation.

I was aware, too, that Hélissenne and Geoffrey had worked together to prepare the volume of the complete correspondence between Abelard and Heloise that I had just finished reading, simultaneously published by leading university presses in France and America, but I had no clue as to what had happened to the original letters themselves.

Canal informed me that, thanks to his connections, he had managed to ensure that Hélissenne was exonerated of all criminal charges, and that the letters had arrived at suitable locations through his own good offices. Not even the later, more legible copy had interested Picard, though not because it occasionally suffered from the scribe's or typist's classic *saut du même au même*, leaving out a couple of lines here and there when the same word or expression appeared in a similar spot further down the page. It simply did not date back to his beloved seventeenth century. Had it been the correspondence between the famed military architect Vauban and the so-called Sun King, Picard, who was a confirmed bachelor as it turned out, would have been delighted to publish them with an elaborate critical apparatus and take full credit for himself.

As it was, however, the sixteenth-century copy had been sent to the regional archives, since it had been at least preliminarily determined to have been transcribed by Marguerite de France, the queen of Navarre, born and raised in Angoulême, and a famous author in her own right, having penned the love stories comprising the *Heptameron*, a takeoff on Boccaccio's *Decameron*. It was not known how she had come into possession of the letters, even if it was possible that Rabelais had had something to do with it, but it appeared from her laconic inscription at the end of them that she had copied them at her writer's retreat in Mont-de-Marsan.

The inspector had, it seemed, pulled numerous strings to ensure that the original twelfth-century manuscript not be sent to the Bibliothèque Nationale or National Archives in Paris but much closer to their fifteenth-century home in Troyes—at the abbey where Jean de la Véprie had originally unearthed them.

"Why," I asked him, "were you so keen on sending the letters to Troyes instead of to Paris?"

"In Paris they would have been buried under tons of other similarly old but hardly as significant documents, contributing simply to the mass of unread, fragile documents available only to library rats, if you say that in English."

Canal knew full well that French was among the languages I spoke, otherwise he would never have referred a single

French-speaking analysand to me these past few years, understanding as he did how important it was for analysands to speak their mother tongue, or at least one of them when they had two or more, while on the couch. I figured, accordingly, that when this man, who spoke English unlike any foreigner I had ever encountered, feigned uncertainty regarding an English idiom he was either checking to see if I was listening—which in this case seemed patent as I had just asked him a question—or testing me to see if my French was as good as I averred. Considering the latter alternative most likely, I enunciated the single word, "Bookworms?"

He smiled cryptically and went on, indicating that in Troyes, on the other hand, the letters would be given pride of place, exposed under glass for all visitors to see, with special lighting and humidity control, of course. It would require a concerted effort on the pilgrim's part to travel to a location not far from where Abelard initially founded his monastery of the Holy Spirit, the Paraclete, and where Heloise established her convent too for many a year. In Paris, the letters would be just one more curiosity, like Heloise and Abelard's gravesites in the Père-Lachaise cemetery, adrift between Apollinaire, Chopin, Champollion, and Jim Morrison.

"There was another detail that intrigued me in your account," I said, affecting nonchalance, motioning to a waiter to bring us another round. "Why did you bother to close the safe after you had gotten it open?"

Canal observed me with renewed interest and appreciation. "I wondered if you would pick up on that particular element," he commented with a sparkle in his eye. "It perhaps takes an analyst or a seasoned detective to file away details like that."

I raised my eyebrows and gestured for him to go on, for it seemed for a moment almost as if he had no intention of telling me why.

He eventually acceded to my request. "I suspected that the thief had not yet been able to open the safe and that he therefore

234

had no idea it did not contain the letters he was seeking. I had had the forethought before leaving Paris for Gincla to bring with me a set of letters that a gifted niece of mine had once prepared as an exercise. Wishing to practice her Latin composition, she had asked whether I had any letters around that she could translate. I thought it would be especially fun for her if she wrote out her French to Latin translations on some old looking parchment paper I had lying about, and gave her a stack of letters that I had written to and received from an older woman I had had an amorous adventure with decades before. She had returned my letters to me when she married 'a more serious man,' as she put it, closer to herself in age," he added, as if the sting had never utterly and completely abated.

"At least she didn't burn your letters, like Gide's wife did," I quipped consolingly.

"Yes, I suppose I should be thankful for that," he remarked meditatively. "My niece," he went on, "was thrilled, since I had both sides of the correspondence, and she could practice her hand at both masculine and feminine styles of expression. Knowing of my proficiency in Latin, she forwarded the letters to me some years later, when Latin was no longer anywhere near the center of her interests, for my perusal and enjoyment.

"As I was packing my things before leaving for the southwest, I thought they might come in handy. I had taken them with me up into the mountains in case they could be substituted for the genuine article at the Cabane de la Balmette and, perceiving the safe to be empty later, I decided to place them in it as a kind of decoy for the burglar, whose command of Latin I suspected was less highly developed than his legerdemain and whose ability to distinguish imitation from genuine twelfth-century parchment I seriously doubted.

"Had he found no letters whatsoever in the safe, he might, I reasoned, go after the two lovers again, meaning that they might be on the run for quite some time. Giving him a decoy would, I thought, likely occupy him, encouraging him to leave

235

the country with the letters as quickly as possible, in the hope of using them in whatever way he thought would be most to his advantage." Canal paused to sip some fine tawny port from the new glasses the waiter had set down before us. "I have no idea what became of the thief, but I suspect that my little smokescreen did the trick."

I scratched my head and pondered this for a few moments. "You didn't bother to have the police come around and book them for breaking, entering, and the like?"

The Frenchman raised his left eyebrow at this. "We had other priorities at the time, and upon reflection Madame Cochenille did not seem terribly keen on pressing charges, which would have inevitably led to still more crime-related news about her establishment getting out." He took another sip from his glass and nodded his head as if approving of the contents. "I generally feel," he added, "that life itself gives such unscrupulous characters their comeuppance without much effort on my part."

I wasn't entirely sure I agreed with his lack of zeal in this sphere, but he went on, "I did take a minute, in the other student's case, to call a rather judicious friend of mine at Harvard. I believe," he continued casually, "that Randolph, who turned out to be an inveterate slacker, was swiftly booted out of the program and effectively blacklisted elsewhere."

This I found rather more satisfying. I smiled and turned to something that had been on my mind for the past few minutes. "If it is not too indiscreet a question," I began, "could you tell me something about this former paramour of yours?"

The inspector was slightly nonplussed by my request, but granted it with good grace, albeit preceded by a disclaimer. "If you are thinking of psychoanalyzing me ...," he said, scrutinizing my features closely, "we are talking here about serious water under the bridge."

"I have a specific aim in view," I told him, knowing full well that any statement couched as a denial—like "I have no such intent"—would be read by him as tantamount to an admission.

He apparently gave me the benefit of the doubt, for he soon uttered, "It was during my very first visit to England. I was staying in London for some time with friends and met a charming woman who spoke rather good French. My spoken English was quite execrable at the time, as you can well imagine, having learned it only from teachers of French origin in junior high and high school. I suppose that I was feeling somewhat off my game in Britain—I thought myself rather witty in France, but found that my sparkling personality did not translate terribly well given my poor command of the language. Hence I was thrilled to meet someone who appreciated my verbal talents and charm."

I nodded in comprehension, having had the experience myself more than once that the primitive puns and other wordplay I was able to invent in only partially acquired foreign tongues were either boring or incomprehensible to my interlocutors, even when they amused me thoroughly.

"She was, moreover, quite a handsome and cultured woman, and I suppose I was somewhat taken with the idea of entangling myself with someone from across the Channel. I intuited right from the outset that it would last but a season, but I have to admit to having been more hurt by her change of heart when it came than I had anticipated."

"I see," I said empathically. I relished learning something at last about the Frenchman's youth, whether dissolute or not, over which he had always seemed to cast an impenetrably thick veil, but I nevertheless continued, "Actually, though, I was wondering if you knew anything about the current identity of this lady friend of yours. Did you keep up with her in any way?"

"We French rarely adopt the 'Can't we just be friends' approach you Americans so often seem to. I never tried to have any further contact with her from the day I received my letters back with a note saying that she had decided to do the 'sensible' thing."

I saw his point and nodded anew.

"Why do you ask?"

"As I think I mentioned to you recently," I responded languorously, taking my sweet time, "although my literary interests were primarily confined to the sixteenth and seventeenth centuries while I was still part of the academic establishment, I have more recently become interested in both older and newer literature, and read every volume of correspondence I can get my hands on, whether by Abelard, Russell, Shaw, or Ruskin—yes, I do even occasionally indulge in nineteenth-century letters, though I strive not to make a habit of it."

"You have to *strive* not to?" he said, winking at me. "Otherwise you might be tempted to make a nasty habit of it?"

We both laughed at this, sharing as we did a marked distaste for most things nineteenth century—excepting detective fiction, to be sure.

"In my trawling for exchanges of letters, I came across a volume published no more than a couple of weeks ago by a Cambridge University student by the name of Bernard Lahron or something like that," I said, monitoring Canal's reaction closely. "It's a highly curious document, providing the Latin text and an English translation of letters that the editor claims were written in the medieval lingua franca between some distant relative of his and an unknown Frenchman many centuries ago."

The inspector was plainly shocked. Perhaps he was wondering whether his sweetheart could possibly have been the grandmother or great aunt of this Lahron—who had lived up to his name in proving to be the thief—the likelihood of which he would be forced to conclude was infinitesimally small. He nevertheless seemed to me at first to be slightly pained, but little by little his face visibly brightened. Twinkling, his eyes soon even began to appear to laugh, if such a thing be possible. "And what press was it that was so injudicious as to print this twentieth-century fabrication?" he asked jocularly.

"One of the Ivy League university presses, naturally," I replied good humoredly.

"So we can be sure it was vetted by at least two *grands pontes*, two bigwigs of the highest academic caliber in classics," Canal commented, beaming broadly as he savored the irony, "who attested to the authenticity of the Latin original, including the grammatical constructions and vocabulary typical of the era."

"Yes," I said, doubling over with mirth, "and who, let us not forget, vouched for the immense historical significance of the document."

The inspector could no longer contain himself now, his glee spilling out in peals of uncontrollable laughter. His hilarity merely fed my own, which already knew precious little restraint. Tears streaming down our cheeks, we continued howling as several club members in adjoining rooms looked in to see what all the commotion was about, turning away as they realized there was nothing to be seen, it being a private joke.

"I guess a letter does at least sometimes arrive at its destination!" Canal eventually quipped, when he had managed to catch his breath.

Recalling the incredibly pedantic to-do a renowned academician once stirred up about the claim a legendary analyst had made that letters *always* arrived at their destination, I burst out laughing anew so hard my stomach soon began to ache, and the inspector's merriment promptly overflowed yet again.

ABOUT THE AUTHOR

Bruce Fink is a practicing Lacanian psychoanalyst and analytic supervisor who trained in France with the psychoanalytic institute Jacques Lacan created shortly before his death, the École de la Cause freudienne in Paris. He has translated several of Lacan's works into English—including *Écrits: The First Complete Edition in English* and *Seminar XX: Encore*—and is the author of numerous books on Lacan, including *The Lacanian Subject, A Clinical Introduction to Lacanian Psychoanalysis, Lacan to the Letter, Fundamentals of Psychoanalytic Technique*, and most recently *Against Understanding* (two volumes).